LATE
TO
LOVE

Print ISBN: 979-8-9888570-7-5

Ebook AISN: B0F3VKS37F

Cover Design & Illustration: Melissa Doughty - Mel D. Designs

Editor: Katie Awdas, Spice Me Up Editing

Published by Stafford Lane Publishing, LLC

For you. Thank you.

CHAPTER 1

DARCY

DAMN, I'M GOOD.

I stand back and look at the lengths of trim, perfectly done. They'll be gorgeous once I sand and stain them.

And, bonus, it'll reduce my rent with Agatha by a little. Which, in this economy? Ya girl needs.

I push my safety goggles to the top of my head and pluck a relatively clean handkerchief from my overalls pocket to wipe the sawdust off my face. The molding cutter is a fantastic tool for my table saw, but it's dirty as all get out.

Now that the trim is finished, I'll get back to the one-of-a-kind dining table I've been working on. I don't have any idea what I'll do with it when I'm done, because my website isn't even up and running yet, but at least I'll have something to sell when the time comes.

"Yoohoo, Darcy!" Agatha's voice carries through the Fleetwood Mac blaring from a speaker I have set up in the garage's corner. I grin. My landlord's here.

Using the remote to turn the seventies mix off, I give the old woman a smile. She is easily the grandmother I never had, and she's not the worst bowler, either. "Hi, Agatha."

She comes farther into the garage, taking in the random pieces of wood, the table saw, the lathe that's almost always being used for one thing or another, and of course, the gorgeous trim I've just completed. To the untrained eye, it may simply look like a standard piece of wood that gets nailed up to the ceiling. But I know that hardly anyone makes their own trim, and this is as personalized and unique as it gets. "Oh, that's lovely!" Her eyes light up as she takes it in.

I preen. See? Agatha knows what's up, even if no one else does. I pull it off the table and hold it up for her inspection. "Thank you."

She runs a hand softly over the unsanded wood. "Really well done, Darcy," she insists. "You should be proud of yourself."

"Aw, thank you, Agatha. I am," I tell her. Too bad my own father isn't as prone to making these types of declarations. I mean, sure, he's proud of me, as well, but for one, he isn't nearly as capable of a carpenter as I am, and for two, my work is rarely good enough for him. He's always pushing me to be better, to do better. I appreciate it, but it's nice to get a simple "good job" every now and then.

Reason number two thousand why I had to move out of the house.

That, and at age twenty-four, I should be living on my own. Not that adulting doesn't suck, because it really does, but at least now I don't have to work a full day with Dad and then be expected to cook while he sits in front of the television with a beer.

I sound ungrateful. Hell, for that matter, it sounds like my dad is some throwback from the 1950s, and it's honestly not the case. He cleaned after I cooked, for one thing. But without another person in the house, the two of us fell into some pretty specific roles as I got older.

"Do you want any of the quiche I made for dinner before we go bowling tonight?" Agatha smooths her wrinkled hands over a teal apron covered in white and pink daisies. I'm obsessed with it and told her so when I moved into the cottage behind her house six months ago, and even though I know she owns more aprons than I do pairs of underwear, this is the one she wears the most.

I nod. "I'd love that. Let me clean up and I'll be over shortly."

She casts a wistful look over the garage as she turns to leave. "It's so good to see this place get the kind of love it deserves."

My heart twinges. She lost her husband when he was too young, only in his early sixties, and all his tools were back here—including the amazing molding cutter—when she allowed me to turn the garage into my personal workshop. I insisted on paying extra for the privilege, and she decided that payment would be made by sprucing up her place with things like the trim I've just finished.

After a hasty shower, I cross the backyard and let myself into the back door. "Here!"

"In the kitchen," she answers.

We make quick work of the simple meal, which is the aforementioned quiche and a side salad tossed in the lightest oil and vinegar dressing imaginable. There's more to the dressing than that, but she refuses to give me her secret. Says it's the same recipe as the Dash In Diner, which I absolutely believe. The owner of the diner, Willa Dash, used to live in my cottage. Then her sister Goldie lived there, and now I do.

To hear Agatha tell it, she's the reason they've both met their respective men, and she is more than happy to turn her attentions to me.

Yeah, no thank you. I adore her, but I won't be trusting Agatha with my love life anytime soon. Not that there's one to speak of, mind you, but still. No way.

After dinner, Agatha rides with me to Hall's Balls, our little town's equivalent of a pool-hall-slash-bowling-alley-slash-bar-slash-arcade. It sits just off the pier and is absolutely packed in the summer with beachgoers and tourists. Given that it's early May, we're mere weeks from being overrun for the season, but the owner is good about letting us keep our weekly slot.

The familiar smell of the place welcomes me as we step inside: a hint of lemon cleaner, followed by an odor I can only classify as the Hall's Balls Special.

We head to the bar at the far end of the space, going past the welcome counter where Harrison usually stands. Someone else is working there instead, and since I don't recognize them, I wave and keep moving.

And there he is.

Anthony Hall. Owner of Hall's Balls and undoubtedly the grumpiest dude to ever grace our small beachside town.

Also the hottest.

He sports a near-constant scowl (hot), a neatly trimmed dark brown beard (very hot), and two delicious sleeves of tattoos (ridiculously hot) over a massive chest that won't quit. He is a specimen of a man, huge in size, and more than once I've fantasized about him tossing me over his shoulder to have his way with me.

But he'd have to actually speak more than ten words a night for me to do anything more than just fantasize about it.

He clocks my and Agatha's arrival and turns to make her usual drink without so much as cracking a smile. Standard.

I half wish I had some gum in my mouth I could snap like a bratty teenager, but alas, I don't. Instead, I flash an overly enthusiastic smile at him when he shifts his attention to me. "Hi, Mr. Hall."

"Anthony." He practically growls it.

I shrug, pretending not to care and delighting in the way his scowl deepens in response.

"Drink?"

I pretend to think about it. Although my order changes

constantly, I always decide beforehand. The delaying tactic is entirely so I can ogle Anthony. And besides, it's fun to irritate him. "Rum and coke, please."

He grunts and turns to make it without another word. I watch him as he works, enjoying the way the black T-shirt is tucked into the delightfully tight jeans he's wearing. Should I be ogling him? Of course not. But he's just so unattainable that somehow it feels okay.

Silently, he slides the drink across the bar, and I wink at him to see if it gets a reaction. Nothing. Well, at least I tried. "Can I start a tab?" I always start a tab, but I always ask.

He raises a brow.

Seriously. One day I'm going to get the man to have an actual conversation with me. I lift my glass. "That's a yes. Thanks!" I wiggle my fingers at him and pivot, beelining for the lane closest to the bar and swapping out my sneakers for bowling shoes. They're personalized, naturally, all black with sparkly red cherries on each side.

A few minutes later, my best friend Amanda shows up, and shortly after that, Devon Joseph appears, making our little team complete. We've been playing for a couple of months now, and while I wouldn't say we're the greatest things since sliced bread, I *would* say we're not nearly as terrible as when we first started.

Progress.

Amanda knocks her glass against mine and sips. "Cheers!"

"Here's to a good session."

"Here's to us finding some cute guys," she corrects.

I laugh. Bowling is not where we're going to find the guys, but whatever Amanda needs to keep this going is good with me. She and I are the single ladies in our little group of four; Devon is married and Agatha's in her early seventies, putting her, and I quote, "so far past wanting another man in my life it's not even funny."

Amanda and I have been best friends since grade school, and

she's been the one to lure the guys in from the second we noticed them. I'm no shrug, but Amanda's got confidence to match her curves, gorgeous smile, and the kindest, most mischievous brown eyes on the planet. She's a knock-out.

Devon is a little older than Amanda and me, in her late thirties and married to a paramedic named Aaron. They moved here from Talladega a couple of years ago for Devon to take a job with the education department down here. I don't know much about it, only that she's a frequenter of the same haunts as me: coffee shop, diner, and Hall's Balls. Of course she needs to be on the team.

With a deep breath, I launch into the spiel I've been working on for the past week. "I think we're ready to participate in a competition. There's one in Mobile, just half an hour away, and it's in three months. If we hunker down and really practice, we can be competitive. What do you think?" I look at them expectantly.

Crickets.

They clearly aren't as excited as me, but I can fix that.

"Dear," Agatha starts gently.

"You're serious?" Amanda asks.

"Let's do it," Devon says brightly.

My shoulders dip with relief. At least I've got one in my corner. "Really?"

Her shoulder-length blond hair bobs as she smiles. "Of course! It'll be fun to have a challenge. Something to look forward to. Besides, we need something to keep us going, making us better, or I'll never get that sweet pink bowling ball that Aaron promised me."

Amanda rolls her eyes. "You and that damn ball."

"It's pretty!" Devon protests.

"Not as pretty as mine," I say, brandishing the cherry-red ball that's been my obsession since starting to bowl a year ago.

Amanda sighs. "Fine. But you're paying the entry fee."

Agatha *tsks*. "I'll pay my portion and Stingy Amanda's over there—but don't think that this means my game will suddenly improve, because I'm not sure that's even possible at my age."

I pull all three of them into a hug, with Amanda protesting loudly. "I love you ladies."

"Yeah, well, let's see how much you love us after we get through ten frames," Devon laughs.

CHAPTER 2

ANTHONY

THE WATER HEATER isn't doing its job again.

I have no one to blame but myself.

Jim warned me I needed to replace it when he was up here last week, but I shrugged him off. How much could the man *really* tell from a five-second glance at the slightly rusting cylinder that looked like it'd seen better days?

Apparently, a lot.

I add it to my mental list of improvements that need to be made to the space I'm now living in, begrudgingly putting it at the very top after taking a bracingly cold shower. Toweling off, I step out of the makeshift bathroom and make the trek across the wide-open loft to the area I've designated as my bedroom. I pull on my usual uniform of jeans and a Hall's Balls black T-shirt. Some socks, a pair of boots, healthy application of deodorant, and a two-minute teeth-brushing session later, I'm heading downstairs to the main portion of Hall's Balls and dialing Jim.

"Awful early for a chitchat," he answers, the knowing *I told you so* grin evident in his tone.

"Water heater's busted," I grunt in response. Why bother with pleasantries with the town's hardware store owner?

"You around today?"

"Jim. I'm *always* around." There are days when I don't even step outside, never mind that the building sits just off the board-walk and I could have my feet on the sand in literal minutes if time allowed.

"We'll get you fixed." He hangs up without another word.

Good man. I appreciate the whole interaction, especially the part where he didn't make me exchange pleasantries. He's one of the few who seems to understand that a person only has so much to say in a day, and if I wanted to talk, I would.

I check my watch. Time to polish the bowling balls and oil the lanes. There are only four of them, but they require nearly the same amount of attention as the rest of the place combined. Granted, there's only so much that the arcade area needs, and Harrison helps with nearly every other aspect of the venue.

The man himself appears around an hour later, after I've tended to the lanes and restocked the bar.

"What's up, boss?" He grins and adjusts his ball cap.

"You need a haircut."

"Says the man with sleeve tattoos," he quips. "Besides, the ladies like it a little unruly. Gives 'em something to hang on to." He gives a devilish smirk as he sidesteps me.

I roll my eyes. Harrison's been working here almost since the day I opened. Doesn't mean he doesn't annoy the absolute shit out of me, though.

It's well past lunchtime when Darcy Belle saunters in, stop-ping to talk with Harrison before making her way to where I'm stationed behind the bar.

"Mr. Hall," she chirps, her cherry-red lips widening into a knowing smile that gets under my skin every time.

"Anthony," I bite out.

She shrugs, the movement serving only to move her blouse up and down against generous breasts. Breasts that I have exactly no business looking at.

She is a child.

Well…she's not a child, but she's around Harrison's age, and whatever age that is, it begins with the number two. Considering my age begins with the number four, I think it's a safe bet that I should keep my eyes the hell off her tits.

Along with the rest of her.

"Mr. Hall suits you." The way it comes out, it seems as though she's had an entire conversation with herself about what, precisely, I should be called and decided that her way—which is the exact opposite of my way—is the winning option.

My jaw ticks.

"How do you want it?" she continues.

I blink.

"The water heater, Mr. Hall." She smirks. "Your place of business is open, and I assume you don't want my guys delivering the water heater through the arcade to get to your loft door. Is there another way? Outside stairs or anything?"

How is it that on anyone else, a bandana wrapped around her hair would look absolutely ludicrous, but on Darcy, it looks perfect? She's like a twenty-first century Rosie the Riveter. I'd never paid too much attention to her until she started coming in to bowl, and suddenly, there was no escaping her. "Stairs outside," I agree.

She smiles brightly. "Excellent! We'll get started." With that, she swivels away from me, hips swaying in denim overalls that I swear were made specifically for her.

I force my gaze elsewhere.

Half an hour later, I find myself upstairs, unable to handle people in my space without supervision.

Darcy. Darcy is people. The guys aren't any big deal, but Darcy can't be left alone up here. I can't explain why. But she can't.

"Mr. Hall." She raises a questioning eyebrow.

"Just wanted to see progress."

"We're installing a water heater, not painting a masterpiece.

But speaking of painting, when did you move in?" She walks into the wide-open loft, casting a dubious gaze across its expanse.

I don't like her tone. "Why." No need to sound curious when I'm not.

She smiles brightly, eyes crinkling, and when she speaks, it sounds as if I've unknowingly walked right into a trap. "Because I think I should handle the renovation."

"What renovation?" To be honest, the place needs about a million years' worth of work. It's simply too overwhelming to think about. I moved into the loft because I was tired of paying rent when I knew there was a perfectly acceptable area up here, and I own this building. Not outright, but still.

"The renovation you clearly need." She walks farther into the sparsely furnished space. "I've got a ton of ideas on how to turn this into a gorgeous, livable home."

"It's already livable. I'm up here, aren't I?" I grumble.

She twirls back to me, her aquamarine eyes glittering. "Aw, Mr. Hall. Do we need to talk about the difference between living in a space and loving the space you live in?"

The hell is she talking about?

She pivots and gasps, walking to the windows. "Holy shit, this view! Sorry. I mean, this view is amazing! How do you not have the entire place configured to maximize it?"

I move toward her, my eyes locked firmly on the incredible view—the one outside, *not* her body. Massive windows overlook the ocean and the white strip of sugary sand just in front of it. There are days when it almost looks fake, like now, when cotton candy clouds dot the cobalt sky and seagulls swoop and dive for their meals.

See? It's so beautiful that it turns me into some kind of poet, talking about cobalt skies and shit. Or maybe Darcy's got me befuddled. Wouldn't be the first time. I clear my throat. "The view is exactly why I bought the building. That, and the fact that it was right on the boardwalk."

She turns to look up at me, and I catch a whiff of her scent. Cherries, maybe? Jesus. I do *not* need to be wondering about this. "You'll let me do it? I'll keep costs low—this will be my first time doing something like this so I'll discount my services, but of course I can't give you any kind of deal on materials—and—"

"Stop." I don't think twice about interrupting her.

She does, but her eyes flash. She did *not* appreciate being told what to do, that's for damn sure.

I don't care. Not when it's about something this important. "Do not ever—and I mean *ever*—discount yourself or your expertise for anyone. Why would you do that?"

Her head jerks back, as if I've slapped her. "Excuse me?"

"You heard me. Consider this a lesson in business." *Though, my God, the other kinds of lessons I could teach her.* "Never offer a discount up front. Your time is valuable. Your expertise is worth something. Don't undervalue it."

A slow, sexy-as-fuck grin spreads across her face. "Why, Mr. Hall, are you saying I'm smart?"

I fight the urge to huff. "I'm saying there's no way I'm paying a discount."

"So that's a yes?" she says hopefully.

"I—" Shit. Did I just get played? I honestly have no idea. "You know what? Fuck it. Sure."

She jumps up and down, clapping her hands.

Do not look at her tits. Do not look at her tits. You are not a creep. Do. Not. Look. At. Her. Tits. My fists are clenched so tight it's a wonder my nails haven't drawn blood on my palms.

"Darcy!" A man's voice hollers from near the water heater. "Think we're all done here. Wanna come check?"

Her eyes slide to me. "Wanna come check?" she repeats. "Since, you know, that's what you came up here for in the first place?"

Brat. She's impossible. And loud, mouthy, and generally a

whirling ball of undeniably sexy chaos any time she's downstairs bowling. How the hell did I just agree to let her into my home?

Sighing, I wave for her to lead the way. And this time, I manage to keep my eyes to myself.

This will all be fine. I need the place to be renovated, that much is true. Did I need it done by someone who drives me crazy? No.

But it's fine. It'll all be fine.

Just fine.

CHAPTER 3

DARCY

I CAN'T BELIEVE he said yes. It's been a week, and I still pinch myself when I remember the conversation. The whole thing was like a fever dream, because I didn't mean to do any of it. But I saw the ocean and suddenly I just *needed* to do it. Before I knew it, I was babbling about discounts and practically begging him to say yes, and he was all growly and *"No discounts"* and honestly, what was I supposed to do? Insist on it because I have quite literally never done something like this?

No way.

The man wants to pay me full freight, then by all means, give me your money, my dude.

My mouth has gotten me into plenty of interesting situations before. Like the time in fourth grade when I bragged about the tree house that was most definitely *not* in the trees in our backyard and declared the whole class should come over for a party, and Todd, the sniveling meanie that he was, totally didn't believe me and said they'd be there on Saturday. Dad wouldn't help me, but he did supervise.

The tree house remains in the back yard. It's almost certainly a safety hazard now, but then? Then, it was a thing of beauty—as much as four walls, a floor, and a crooked roof could be. How no one commented on the new-wood smell that weekend is beyond me.

I still think about the look on Todd's face when he saw that I actually had a tree house. God, it was good.

Anyway, here I am again, in another self-made situation that I'm absolutely unprepared for, in a loft I would probably murder someone to live in, figuring out how to move forward. He's barely touched the place, that much is obvious. But it's clean. No dusty corners, no grimy windows. He cares about his home, even if he hasn't done anything with it. Something about it is, I don't know, touching? It's weird. I can't describe it.

"Where should we put this?" Jeff holds one side of the drywall while his partner Kevin holds the other.

I point to the long expanse of blank wall along the east side of the building, and the guys head there. Once I'm sure they know where to put the stacks of drywall, I turn back to inspect the space. I have so many ideas. Ways to separate the open areas into something warm and inviting. I may have bulldozed my way in here, but honestly, it's a dream to get to design this. It's so far out of my comfort zone that it's in another country, but a girl's gotta start somewhere, right?

I scoff. My dreams are so big that sometimes I don't know how I'll ever find the time to make them all come true. Because it's not just the furniture and custom trim that I'm interested in. It's full-on design and bespoke items that are meant to fit one space and one space only. Heirlooms for families. Pieces that matter. I love a good Ikea bookshelf as much as the next girl, but there is nothing better than staining a set of shelves that you've worked hard to build yourself. I have no business doing a full-on renovation of someone's loft, but if you think that's going to keep me from doing it, you clearly haven't met me.

After Kevin and Jeff finish their delivery and leave, I inspect the kitchen—maybe more thoroughly than is strictly necessary, but hey, do you blame me?—and head to the bathroom. As I'm washing my hands, I decide to do the very thing that, were I a girlfriend, I would never do. Or probably wouldn't do. Maybe I would. Hell, I don't know. Either way, I take a little tour of the grumpy man's medicine cabinet.

The damn thing creaks when I open it, the stupid rusty hinges. I squawk like I'm about to get caught, then peek out of the pitiful excuse for a door to make sure that Anthony hasn't shown up.

Coast is clear.

Back to snooping.

Yes, I can totally admit I'm snooping. Of course I am. But since I'm not an unhinged girlfriend, that's okay, right? No shade to unhinged girlfriends. In fact, let's not call them unhinged. We'll say they're…over-invested.

Toothbrush, whitening toothpaste for sensitive teeth, some ibuprofen, Q-tips, and ooh, what's this? Beard oil.

With zero hesitation, I grab it, twisting the lid off and bringing it to my nose to sniff. *Whoa.* This smells amazing. Like a winter bonfire on the beach. Bet it's even more amazing when it's on the man himself.

"Darcy?"

Shit.

I screw the lid back on and shove the oil onto the tiny shelf, then pray to the gods that the door doesn't squeak when I close it. It's quiet, thank goodness. Then I flush, again, and wash my hands a second time to keep the ruse going.

Opening the flimsy door, I flash Anthony a bright smile. "Mr. Hall!"

He frowns. "Anthony."

God, it's ridiculously fun to annoy him. I shrug. "I like Mr. Hall better. Let's not rehash it."

His frown deepens, and honestly, I didn't know that was possible. "What are you doing in there?"

I tilt my head. "What was I doing in the bathroom? What do you *think* I was doing in there?" I consider waving my hands in his face and asking him if he wants to smell them, then reconsider. He'd probably lose his mind.

Also, that's gross. I wouldn't want anyone doing that to me.

He makes a noise that sounds suspiciously like a grunt, then turns away from me. "What is all this?"

"The drywall? It's…drywall." I follow him to the kitchen. It's the only area that's clearly seen some updating, but it's still in desperate need of some design love.

With his back to me, he reaches to grab a glass from the cabinet, and the movement serves to bring my focus entirely on the way his T-shirt rides up, revealing the tiniest strip of skin above his jeans.

Damn, Mr. Hall is giving some serious ass. It's not as noticeable behind the bar because it's dark down there, but up here, where the sun is streaming and I'm not waiting on a drink, there's nothing to do but watch this behemoth of a man move around his kitchen.

Our eyes meet when he faces me again, and I snap my mouth shut—because clearly I was this close to drooling—and I think… was he…?

Did his eyes do what I think they did?

No. No way. Anthony Hall isn't interested in me. And I don't think I'm interested in him. Not *really*. Unless I am.

That's probably not the best idea since I'm going to spend the next few months working in his loft.

Eh, good ideas are overrated. Why be cautious when you're twenty-four?

Okay, that's such a lie. I have spent my entire life being cautious. Hard not to when you learn to wield a saw before you're three feet tall. And being raised by an overprotective yet remarkably oblivious father who would sooner put me in a bubble than see me do anything that could harm me. Are those two things a little opposed to each other? Yes. But Jim Belle is a man of contradictions, and I am his unwilling victim.

It's one of the many reasons I moved out of our house. That, and if I ever want to prove to him that I have what it takes to make it on my own, then I need to get out from under his wing.

"Water?"

"Huh?" *Wow, Darcy. Excellent conversational skills.*

"Would you like some water?" Anthony holds the glass out for me. And it's actual glass, too, nothing like the plastic cheap cups I got for five for a dollar at the Dollar General when I moved into the cottage behind Agatha.

I take it, admiring the pattern cut into it: one row of diamonds surrounded on both sides by smaller diamonds, then parallel lines cut around the glass for even more texture. It's a dusty rose color, too, something I wouldn't have placed in this man's house if you held a nail gun to my head.

"Thanks."

We drink and stare at each other for longer than is polite. When I realize what's happening, I blink and look away. He clears his throat and busies himself with getting his own glass of water.

Have I mentioned how sexy smelling that beard oil was? And why am I thinking about it when I should be drinking my water and getting on with it?

"Shouldn't you be downstairs? Working?" I emphasize the last word.

He tilts the glass up to empty it, and how is it that the man freaking *swallowing* is hot? Shit. I am unwell.

The glass hits the counter with a *clink* and his eyes narrow. "I told you, I wanted to check on things up here."

I push off the counter and set my now-emptied glass in the sink. *See? You may set your glass on the counter, but here I am, going one better and putting mine in the sink. So there.* "You've checked. Now leave. I have things to do."

I sway my hips more than strictly necessary as I walk away,

confident he's watching. I'm a curvy girl, and even in overalls, I'm well aware of what I've got to work with.

Behind me, I hear his grunt of frustration and bite back a smile. The man is beyond fun to irritate.

But also? I might want a little more than to just mess with him. He's older than me—at least ten years, but maybe more, it's hard to tell—but why not? He's hot as hell, and something tells me he'd be a lot of fun in bed. Those tattooed arms wrapped around me as he flattened me into the mattress? Yes, please.

After he's gone and I'm deep in concentration, measuring the space and brainstorming on how to make it cozy, my dad calls.

"Hey, Dad." I put the phone on speaker and toss it onto the floor beside me. "What's up?"

"Just checking on you."

I bristle. What is it with these men and the need to check in on me? I'm not a child. "Everything's fine. Doing the job." It's nearly impossible to keep the annoyance out of my voice.

"Good, good. How is it over there? Anthony being nice?"

"Anthony is working. Same as me." When has this man ever wanted to be this involved? The answer is never. But in fairness, he's never been the one to do any kind of interior work. He owns the hardware store. I'm the one who insisted on learning how to use damn near every tool in the store. I'm the one who insisted on building an infinite number of bird houses, then mailboxes, then flower boxes, and on and on, until I was smelling of sawdust instead of the beach like the rest of my grade school friends. I have never been on par with most people my own age—not when I was a kid, and certainly not now. "But it's wide open and beautiful," I answer. "Lots of space to do just about anything he'll let me do."

"When will you be coming by the store? I have some invoices I need your help with. The software's giving me trouble."

"I've shown you what to do, Dad. You have to pay attention next time."

"Why pay attention when I know you're going to do it?" he jokes.

Yeah, it's not funny. I've explained that I'm working to get my own shop off the ground, but I don't think he's really let it sink in. Like, at all. I've always worked with Dad, and it was only recently that I started thinking that maybe, just maybe, it was time to branch off on my own. Not that I'm ready to do it just yet, and not that Dad's ready to hear it.

Sighing, I say, "I'll be there soon. I'm in the middle of things over here. Talk to you later."

CHAPTER 4

ANTHONY

"THANKS FOR COMING." I stand, and the kid's eyes widen a bit before he stands and stammers a thank you, then turns and bolts before I can so much as round the desk.

I swear the kids get younger and stupider. I make a note to call him later and tell him he's got the part-time job for the summer, then wipe a hand down my beard. It's been the week from hell, and to make matters worse, it's Thursday. Which means it's Darcy's bowling league's night.

Although, the word "league" is a little strong to describe the absolute atrocity that is the team's abilities. But it's not my place to judge. I make sure their lane is always reserved and keep my opinions to myself, no matter how much I want to correct every bad move they make. Locals keep the place open through the winter, and even as we're kicking into summer, my job is to make sure they have everything they need. Nothing more, nothing less.

The past week has been far more challenging than I thought it would be. Darcy is fucking everywhere. *Everywhere.* She's up in the loft before I can finish my coffee, despite my repeated requests for her to come later, and I swear she is all I can smell.

Like summer-ripe watermelon and cherries and *God dammit*, I need it to stop.

I stalk through Hall's Balls, checking out the individual areas as I go. The office is behind the welcome area at the front of the building. Right next to it are the pinball machines and other games geared for the smaller set, and then two Skee-ball lanes. Across from that area and down a bit are the five pool tables. They tend to get going later in the day, after the game area empties out, meaning I never have to worry about the little kids annoying the pool players or the pool players being scary to the littles. Next up is my bar, which is where I'm usually stationed. I can see the whole place from behind there, and that's exactly how I like it. Restrooms are across from the bar. Then the bowling lanes, four of them, to the left of the bar, and a couple of party rooms across from the lanes.

I love this place. I have put my heart into it for the past decade, and love everything about it. It may not be the snazziest, or the coolest one with the most up-to-date games and latest ways to take visitors' money, but it's mine. The building is on its way to being mine, too.

That's my only comfort right now as I take my place back behind the bar as the evening kicks into gear. I've already stocked the beer and any liquor that needed it, and of course, the bar itself is wiped down and as clean as can be. You can't have a family game center and have a gross bar; it won't work like that.

A familiar figure in blue slides onto the stool out of the corner of my eye, and I turn to see my brother Ox, Lucky's chief of police. He grins. "Hey, big brother."

I nod in response, my lips tilting into enough of a smile that he knows I'm happy to see him.

His grin only broadens in response. "There it is! That's a huge smile. *Huge.* I can see those pearly whites and everything!" he jokes.

"Shut up," I respond.

"Is that how you talk to your patrons?" Aaron Joseph, one of our paramedics and the husband of a woman on Darcy's bowling team, laughs as he takes his spot next to Ox.

"It is now," I grumble, but it's hard to keep a straight face when Ox is around. He's always been the joker of the family, and thank God for it.

"He's just mad that he ended up the oldest and ugliest," Ox quips.

Aaron laughs, nodding a thanks as I slide a draft beer in front of him. He'll have one beer and then switch to water so that his wife can be the one to have a few drinks. "As the baby of three boys, I understand."

"You've got two brothers?" Ox asks. "Where are they?"

"Up in Talladega," comes the answer. "One's the fire chief up there, and the other runs a bed-and-breakfast—but he used to be a fireman as well."

"Tell them drinks are on me if they ever visit." I slide the margarita across the bar as soon as Aaron's wife appears.

"Thanks, Anthony," she says with a smile.

"Devon, how are you?" Ox asks. "Do you get the summer off?"

She snorts a laugh. "No way. I'm the school system administrator. I don't get summers off. A well-deserved vacation here and there, but definitely not the same kind of break that a teacher gets."

Agatha and Darcy are next, ambling up from the front. Agatha is my chardonnay patron—I keep bottles of the decent stuff for her and her alone—and Darcy? She changes her order all the fucking time. Because of course she does. Why make things easy for me?

The closer she gets, I can see that she's showered and changed from when I saw her just two short hours ago. She wears a fitted cheetah-print skirt and a patterned button-down shirt that ties at the waist, giving me a tantalizing glimpse of soft belly with every step she takes.

Dammit. I can't catch a break with this woman.

Her lips are stained their usual cherry red, and her dark hair hangs loose and wavy around her shoulders, which makes me nearly swallow my tongue. Because I'm not sure I've ever seen her hair completely down. And thank fuck I haven't, because I probably would have been a goner long before now.

She's fucking adorable.

And the smile she tosses at me, as though she's perfectly aware of how edible she looks, is enough to make my jeans tighten. "Mr. Hall."

And *that* is another thing. I can't have her calling me that. All it makes me think of is how it would sound coming out of her mouth as I pound into her from behind, pressing her against the brick wall upstairs, hearing her pant as I dig my hands into her soft ass. "Anthony."

Her grin morphs into a smirk. "No drink ready for me?"

I scowl. "You change your order too much for me to know what you want." Even though I'm fairly certain I know what she's going to order, I wait.

She tilts her head and taps her chin, like she's thinking. "You're right. I do. Let's go with...rum and coke, please." A pause. "With cherries. Lots of them."

I knew it. Holding back a satisfied smirk, I make her drink. When I slide it over to her, she wraps those red lips around a cherry and sucks it into her mouth, and I swear to fucking God she knows exactly what she is doing to me. If she doesn't, then I'm a damn alligator.

"Ready?" she asks the girls. That includes her fourth teammate and woman I think is her best friend, Amanda. Sweet girl. Vodka soda with lemon.

They take off to their reserved lane, which is always the one closest to the bar. I make sure it's the best oiled, too—not that any of them would know that, and not that they need to. They're terrible at the game, and their form is heinous, but the least I can do is give them a slick lane.

Does that sound dirty as hell? Yeah. But whatever.

Aaron turns from watching Devon walk away and tips his beer at me. "Cheers."

I nod.

"So, you're the oldest?"

"Ox has a twin."

Aaron looks at my brother, eyes wide as he smiles. "Holy shit —there are two of you? How did I not know that?"

Ox preens under the attention. "My brother Levi lives in New Orleans. He's married. Living his best life."

I barely suppress a chuckle. Ox isn't wrong, but the look of pure jealousy on his face is something to behold. I know he wants his own person to love, and it's hard in a town as small as ours. Hell, Levi met his future wife when he was in law school. It's probably worse for Ox, though, because he's chief of police. I have no idea if him being only into guys makes it harder or easier, frankly, because I have never asked. It's not my place.

Aaron smiles ruefully. "I get it, man. Talladega's a small town, too. Hard to find your person, isn't it?"

Ox crunches a piece of ice. "Anyway," he says, turning to me, "we have to talk about Mom and Dad's anniversary party. Which is also Dad's retirement party."

I pin my brother with a glare. "What is there to talk about? They want a party. Done."

"Are *you* planning it?"

I grimace. "Absolutely not."

He slides his glass toward me for a water refill. "See, you think you're not planning it, but actually, you're helping me and Levi."

"No."

"Oh, come on, Anthony!" he pouts. "You're the oldest. Shouldn't this be your job, anyway?"

"Whining doesn't suit you." I don't bother saying what I really feel, which is that our parents pretty much never bothered making a big deal out of anything for us, so why should we do something this big for them?

Whatever.

"Look," Ox says, "I know you don't want to be involved. You never do. But for this, you have to be. This is a team sport. You're on the damn team, brother."

"Just tell me where to send my money," I huff.

"It's going to be epic," he declares, spreading his arms. "I want a live band, we'll invite all Dad's former students—"

"How the hell are you going to do that?" I brace my hands on the polished oak of the bar.

"Social media, my dude. You've heard of it?"

Aaron laughs and takes a sip of his beer. "Ox, I don't think Anthony here cares one bit about this."

"He has to!" Ox protests. "They're our parents!"

The phrase makes me stiffen. Which, obviously, it shouldn't. I just...try not to think of my parents that often. Sure, they're in the same town as me, but I don't go see them and they certainly don't come here to see me. We're not a Sunday dinner kind of family.

We were when we were kids, though. But we didn't have a choice. Mom said we'd all eat at least one dinner a week together, and Sunday was the one that always worked. You'd think that we could have made more happen, and we did for years, but once all three of us were in football, life was a lot busier than even our dad anticipated—and he was a chemistry teacher at the high school. It worked out well so that he could always make sure we got rides home if we needed it, but I made sure to get rides with my buddies the second they got cars, and my brothers did the same when their friends hit the same age, too.

Ox studies me, his keen eyes assessing far more than people usually give him credit for. He's loud, lovable, and boisterous, but none of that means he's not smart as the devil. Both my brothers are. I got the height; they got the smarts. I mean, hell, Levi's a lawyer who made millions in Manhattan before coming back down south. And Ox is our police chief. Obviously, he's intelligent.

But right now, I wish he'd put that brain of his to a different use. I'm not interested in being analyzed.

"You want a drink or what?" I ask him.

He blinks, then offers me his standard "make the people happy" smile. "Nah, but thanks. I'll get with Levi, and we'll let you know what we decide. Sound good?"

"Perfect."

"Thought so." He slaps Aaron on the back. "Good to see you, man."

"Next time," Aaron replies, raising his pint glass in salute. His attention is back on me as Ox takes his leave. "You're the oldest?"

I nod.

Aaron nods knowingly. "It's uncanny how much you remind me of my oldest brother, Will. He's just as grumpy as you, but you're bigger." He chuckles. "Then again, you're bigger than just about anyone. What are you, anyway?"

"Six-four."

"Big motherfucker." He grins as he slides off the stool. "I'm gonna go check on the girls."

My head's a fucking mess as he leaves. It feels like everyone has such clarity around what they want, what they feel. And I've always known what I wanted: first was to not be hungry. Second was to never again live in a trailer park for as long as I lived. And those things happened the second I left home for college and started playing football for The University of Alabama. But it turns out that getting everything you want only goes so far.

Darcy chooses that precise moment to saunter back up to the bar. "How's it going, Mr. Hall?"

I stare at her. She's fucking beautiful. Thank God people are used to me being a prick, because it lets me take my fill of her without having to apologize for it.

She goes onto her tiptoes and leans her forearms on the bar, tilting towards me and giving me an unobstructed view down her button-up. I catch a hint of black lace and immediately have to fight the urge to toss her over my shoulder and take her upstairs to have my way with her.

She is a child, Anthony. Remember, she is a child.

When I force my gaze up to hers, her smile is nothing short of mischief. As if she knew exactly what she was doing when she positioned herself like that, and I fell right into her trap.

Brat.

"You want a drink?"

She blinks slowly, her feral grin growing as she lets her eyes roam the rows of bottles behind me. I don't bother hiding that I'm staring at her. She wants me to, and I want to. It's dangerous as hell, and I should absolutely stop, but I absolutely will *not* stop.

"Yes."

I hold back an amused laugh, because of course she wants another one. This entire interaction was never about the drink, and we both know it.

I pull the cocktail together, well aware that she wants a ton of cherries in it again, and well aware that she's the only one I'd do this for. When I finally turn around, nerves frayed beyond comprehension, she jerks her eyes back up to mine. She was absolutely looking at my ass.

"You played for Alabama, right?" she asks as I slide the drink over to her and take her card in return.

I give a quick jerk of my head and a grunt in the affirmative.

"Position?"

You over my knee while I spank you. "O-line." I slide the card back to her.

"O-line?"

I have no business saying what I'm about to say. Leaning closer and lowering my voice, I answer. "O-line. Offensive line. My job was to take down anyone and everyone and put them on their back, by any means necessary. Lots of crouching. Lots of lunging and pushing. It's very physical. With all the crouching, and lunging. You might even call it a thrust sometimes, the way I had to move." Her eyes are blown, pupils dilated and hazy, and I know I have her exactly where I want her.

Which is why I need to stop.

I snap to my full height, and as she blinks those doe eyes of hers, they come alive with mischievous delight.

"I see," she answers. "Very interesting. Maybe I should pay more attention to the sport."

"Maybe. Maybe not." I tap her card to pull her attention off me. I never ran it. "Drink's on the house. Your money's no good here."

She frowns. "Why?"

"Because you're working for me."

She slides the card into the tiny clutch she carries and gives me a pleased grin. "Maybe I'll have another, then."

I shake my head. "You have a job to do in the morning."

She hums and twirls around, walking slower than she needs to, plush hips swaying.

That girl is trouble.

The problem? I like trouble.

Chapter 5

Darcy

IT'S THE FIRST Saturday in June, and on any other normal time, I'd be making plans with my bestie Amanda to pack up and spend the entire day at the beach. But because I'm determined to get this project done on time and on budget, I'm letting myself into Hall's Balls far too early in the day for the place to be open. Earlier even than I've come during the week, because I woke up early and figured I may as well get this done.

Obviously, Anthony did not give me a key to the main building. Obviously, I already had one from working at the town's only hardware and key-making store. We have copies of all the merchant's keys, which is probably weird, but it's been this agreed-upon thing for so long that I rarely stop to think about it.

Making a note to figure out why Anthony's fire escape door wasn't one of the keys we had to copy, I open the door leading up to his loft. It's dark in the small hallway, which makes sense; the only light fixture is from the loft. Which needs to be fixed, and it's so easy to do that I add it to my list.

Knocking on the door, I wait for any kind of answer: a grunt, a yell, or, even better, a door opening and a smiling Anthony waiting on the other side.

Yeah, that's delusional.

I try again, but after no response, I finally try the knob. It's open. Stepping over the threshold, I determine that he's probably not even here. With the way that man looks, he's probably running on the beach like a madman. Or lifting weights in the corner of the loft with earbuds in and music so loud he'd never hear me.

I'm a few steps in and heading toward the kitchen when the floor shakes with footsteps. I turn, and there's Anthony.

Almost entirely naked.

Wrapped only in a white towel that hangs low and loose on his hips, showing off that delicious dip between hip and heaven.

Holy. Fuck.

I shouldn't stare. I should absolutely look away, but there is no way I'm doing that. Not even close. I couldn't stop gaping at him if I tried.

I might be drooling.

His arms are covered in tattoos that go up and over his front shoulders, gracing his unbelievably huge chest as they give way to a thin layer of dark hair. And so help me, I have never thought a hairy chest was sexy, but I'm changing my mind effective immediately. The magnitude of him, the sheer *breadth* of him, is on full display as he stops and regards me, an expression of surprise flitting across his face moments before he schools it into something else.

"Miss Belle," he smirks. He *smirks*.

Wait. Is Anthony Hall actually…flirting with me? No way. He would never.

Unless he would.

"I…" Yep, still unable to talk. Good job by me.

"Quit staring," he snaps, his voice sharp but also…hot?

I shake my head, forcing myself out of the near-catatonic state his body put me in, and blink rapidly. "Sorry." My cheeks are on fire. Why is it that sometimes I feel completely in control of the conversation with him, and other times, I'm absolutely on my metaphorical back?

Not that I wouldn't mind him putting me on my physical back.

He resumes his path toward the bedroom, calling out as he goes, "You should be."

I press my hands to my face, desperate to cool off. I can't believe I just saw what I saw. I can't believe I stared at him like a total pervert. I can't believe how fucking *hot* he is.

"Coffee's made." His voice carries easily across the expanse. "May as well pour yourself a cup since you're helping yourself to everything else in my house."

Shit. I know he's trying to embarrass me, and in many ways it's working. My pride won't quit, though, so pour a cup of coffee I do. Maybe the scalding temperature will get me back in a working state of mind. But when he emerges from his bedroom and finds me in the kitchen, clad in gray sweatpants and a ratty white T-shirt, I nearly sink to my knees.

The man is entirely unfair.

He's. Wearing. Gray. Sweatpants. Come. *On.*

A gleam of something approaching playfulness sparks in his eyes. "Figured I may as well help you."

"You don't have to do that."

"Yeah, well, you didn't have to break into my home at seven a.m. on a Saturday morning, but here we are," he shoots back.

I throw my shoulders back. Nope. He's not making me feel bad about this. "I'm committed to getting this done. On time and on budget."

He snorts an amused laugh, but it's not unkind. "Darcy. The only time a project is done on time is if the person lies about how long it's going to take in the first place. And even then, it's up for grabs."

"Not on my watch." God, I hope I can stick to that.

"Uh-huh." His eyes dance over the rim of a coffee cup. "What are we doing today, boss?"

Boss? I swallow. Guess we're really doing this. Fuck me. Here's hoping I don't slice a finger off with as distracted as he's going to make me. "First, we get some music going." I take the speaker out of my tote, followed by my phone.

"Oh no," he says, stepping forward. "I'm in charge of the music today." He pulls his phone out of his sweatpants—and thank God, because they were threatening to slide lower and I'm not sure if I could have behaved enough to keep my eyes to myself. No idea if he's wearing underwear with those pants, but if he is, they're not doing much to, um, *contain* him. Because… yeah.

It's hot in here.

In moments, he's paired his phone with the speaker and the sound of Noah Kahan streams out. It's a perfect complement to the overcast weather outside, and I can't stop the look of surprise on my face.

"What?"

I grin. "Nothing. Just…didn't take you for a Noah Kahan fan."

"There's a lot you don't know about me, Darcy. Despite snooping through my medicine cabinet." He winks and turns away, leaving me gaping after him.

Holy *shit*. He's funny and playful. I have never seen this side of him. And then I realize something else: He's *talking*. Like, not just speaking in one-word sentences or grunting at me when I ask something. Talking.

Also—he totally knows I went snooping in his medicine cabinet. Whoops.

With another sip of my coffee—which is delicious, by the way, he had the perfect creamer and I knew exactly where the sugar was—I hustle after him. "We're installing trim today."

He nods, his gaze finding the stack of custom trim I've spent the past week making in the few spare hours I have between this job and helping Dad at the store. "Over there?"

"Yep."

His long stride eats up the distance as he nears the stack, then pulls one out to look at it. "I don't know shit about this stuff, but this doesn't look like store-bought."

I don't bother hiding my smile. "Because I made it." Stepping closer, I say, "That's a larger trim than you'd find in a normal store. Trim is a total luxury for a space this huge, but I knew I could do it for a good price, and I thought it'd go a long way towards making it feel homey. Getting up there to install it is another thing entirely, so I'm actually glad you decided to help today. That way, I don't have to fear for my life when I go up this ten-foot ladder."

But he's staring at me when I turn back to him. "You…made this?"

I shrug. "Yeah. It's not like it's hard."

His eyes bug out. "It's hard, Darcy. It's very hard. Don't put yourself down like that."

Damn him. Because that makes me feel things I shouldn't. Things like him being more than hot. Things like, I could really be into this man, and that's a bad idea.

Such a bad idea.

"You ready?" I say instead. "We'll start in the kitchen. That's the smallest area and we'll feel like we're really accomplishing something once it's done."

Without waiting on an answer, I get set up, strapping my tool belt around my waist and looking up in time to catch a hint of something in his eyes that I can't quite place. Does Anthony have a tool girl kink?

Scratch that. The man is significantly older than me. He's guaranteed to have kinks I probably don't even know exist.

"You're going to hold the ladder while I get up there, then hand me the first piece when I ask, okay?"

He nods wordlessly. Which is good.

I shimmy up the ladder, forcing myself to forget everything except the job at hand, and position myself in the perfect spot to nail the first piece of trim. "Hand it up."

A long, five-foot piece of trim comes into view as I pop some nails between my lips. Grabbing it, I nestle the wood into place and keep it steady with one hand, then pull my nail gun out of my tool belt with my other. One well-placed aim later, the first nail is in. I stretch to the right to get the next nail in, then reach the opposite way to get the third. That's enough to keep the trim in place while I move positions, so I put the gun in my belt and climb down.

"Let's move to the right," I instruct Anthony, who's remained incredibly quiet during this entire portion of the morning. He does as requested, and we repeat the pattern. In no time at all, we've got the kitchen done.

"There." With no small amount of satisfaction, I stand back to inspect my work. The trim is tight against the ceiling, the nails invisible to the eye from down here already, and of course, I'll putty over them to smooth the surface before they get painted.

"Looks good," Anthony remarks. "How long would it have taken you without me here?"

"Longer," I laugh. "That's all you need to know. Ready for more?"

His eyes flash, and I swear he's thinking something dirty. "Sure."

"Time for a music change, though." I throw on an 80s mix, and his lip curls in amusement.

"How old do you think I am, Darcy?"

Laughing as I make my way to the next area of the loft we're going to focus on, I answer, "Your age has nothing to do with what I chose to put on. I like this music. But for the record, I have no idea. Fifty? Fifty-three?" I'm ribbing him, and when I turn to him, his jaw is wide open.

"What?" he sputters. "You don't honestly think I'm that old, do you?"

I grin. "I don't know, Mr. Hall. Why don't you tell me?"

There goes that flash of heat in his eyes again. I think he hates me calling him that because he *loves* me calling him that. Wonder what would happen if I called him Daddy?

"I'm forty-one." He delivers it in a gruff voice, as if he's both proud of the number but also maybe a bit embarrassed.

"Forty's a great decade," I shoot back. "Or so I've heard from my grandfather."

His mouth quirks, and something suspiciously like a laugh comes out when he says, "You little brat."

I should get an award for how diligently I ignore the almost-smile, the almost-laugh, and the word he used. Because my insides just turned to lava. "C'mon. Bring the ladder over here." I point him in the direction I want, then head to grab more trim.

Forty-one years old. He's seventeen years older than me.

It's way hotter than it should be.

CHAPTER 6

ANTHONY

I'M NOT SAYING I'm disappointed that Darcy didn't show up again today.

But…maybe I'm a *little* disappointed. I check the time. Reid's texted me yet again about going to yoga, and even though I'm positive I'll look like a complete and total ass, I figure, why the hell not.

Throwing on a pair of old shorts and a fitted tank—which Reid told me I'd want unless I wanted my shirt hanging in my face during some of the positions, which, frankly, almost made me second-guess the entire thing—I take off at a brisk walk. It's probably ten minutes at the most, given that the studio is at one end of the pier and Hall's Balls is at the other.

Reid's waiting for me when I get there, his black cat Midnight strapped to his chest in a baby carrier or something. It's absolutely ridiculous, but I've given him hell about it enough that it no longer fazes him. Not that it ever did. It makes sense, I suppose; the guy moved to town after working undercover with a Miami drug cartel for years. If the man wants to wear a cat because it brings him joy, who am I to tell him no? The dude has seen plenty in his lifetime.

He smiles broadly. "Wondered when I'd finally talk you into this. What changed your mind?"

"Figured it was the only way you were ever going to shut up about it," I grin back.

He slaps my shoulder and gestures for me to go in ahead of him. "You're right. We've got you set up with a mat next to us toward the back."

I nod to the owner, Samantha, who gives me a warm smile in return.

"Anthony Hall! Never thought I'd see you here. First class is always free. Take it easy and I'll make sure you don't overdo it, okay?"

"Sure thing." But how hard can yoga actually be? I work out. I run. This is bending and shit. Piece of cake.

Willa waves to me and I make my way toward her, nodding to Goldie and Matty as I go.

"You're here," Willa says, indicating the mat in front of her. "We would have put you beside one of us, but there's no room."

We say our hellos and I realize that not only has Reid let Midnight down to walk among the mats, but Matty's dog, Killer, is also running around. "Is this allowed?" I ask, eyeing the little chihuahua as he saunters up to sniff at my feet.

"Mr. Hall, what a surprise."

I look up and double-take, because there, in front of me, is Darcy. In a pair of fitted shorts that molds to her luscious ass and a top that bares most of her creamy stomach. The shorts nip in at her flesh, and I fight to hold back the groan that begs for release. "Anthony," I grit out, my name the only thing I trust myself to say right this moment.

She brightens. "No, I'm Darcy. *You're* Anthony." Her saucy grin tells me she knows exactly what she's doing.

Brat. It's on the tip of my tongue to say it again, but I keep it to myself. "You...do yoga?"

"Starting to. I've never seen you here, though—how long have you done it?"

"First time."

Reid joins us, slapping me on the back yet again. "I've been trying to get Grumpy Gus here for months. I finally wore him down."

Darcy snorts as Samantha calls the class to order, and as I look around to figure out what I'm supposed to do, she leans over from the mat beside me. "Just go slow. Don't force anything, and feel free to watch me if you need to see how to get into position."

It's impressive, the way she can say sentences like that without blushing. I nod once, determined not to look at Darcy at all if I can help it, and turn my attention back to Samantha.

Exactly five minutes later, I'm mentally cursing Reid. Because this is absolute torture. I am not limber by any stretch of the imagination, and it turns out that yoga requires a shitload of that.

I can do this. I *will* do this. I won't be beaten by something as easy as yoga.

Ten minutes later, I've changed my tune. Samantha's voice is probably meant to be soothing as she says, "And fold up, arms swinging high overhead, exhale as you lower your arms to your side. Good. Now turn your entire body so that your feet are facing the wall on the right, then spread your legs wide, hands on your hips. Inhale. On that exhale, bend over at the waist, keeping your spine straight as you lower the top of your head to the floor."

Lower the top of my head to the *floor*? She's got to be fucking kidding. But I turn into position anyway and immediately groan. Because in front of me is Darcy's gorgeous butt, right at eye level as I attempt to keep my spine straight.

"Bend a little more, Mr. Hall," Darcy teases in a low voice.

I startle, then realize that she's looking at me from between her legs as she rests the top of her head on the floor, smirking. She definitely caught me looking where I shouldn't.

Fuck. Me.

I did *not* need to know how flexible Darcy is.

Ever.

Does she look a little crazed, the way she's giving this maniacal grin at me, blood rushing into her face? Yes. But also: her ass and thighs are right. Fucking. There.

I'm a pervert.

My cheeks blaze as I avert my eyes and try to do more than look like an overgrown baboon, but it's pretty bad.

I spend the entire ninety minutes in a state of tortured panic. Torture because yoga is, it turns out, hard as fuck, and panicked because Darcy herself is hot as fuck.

It's not a great combination for me right now. I'm fully aware that everyone is here for their mental and physical health. They most definitely are not here to be leered at. But try telling that to my eyes, who can't stop glancing at Darcy and imagining whether any of these yoga positions can be converted into sex positions.

I know. I'm a terrible human being.

When class ends, I'm a sweaty, sore, mentally fucked in the head mess. I beeline for the front, my rolled-up mat in my hands to give to Samantha as I shove my feet back into my sneakers.

"What did you think?" she asks, her voice chipper and a little too interested.

"He did great," Reid says. "Didn't he, Willa?"

Willa nods enthusiastically. "Way better than the first time I came, Anthony. You should have seen me. I couldn't even touch my toes—and you were killing those one-legged balance poses!"

Uh-huh. Whatever. All I do is nod and jerk my thumb to the outside. "See you out there." I need out of here. Away from yoga, and definitely away from Darcy and that tight, royal-blue outfit she's wearing.

I gulp in the salty air, never more grateful for the ocean breeze than I am right now. Behind me, people stream out in a chorus of goodbyes, and of course, my ears strain to hear the one woman's voice I'm desperate for.

"Not bad, Mr. Hall," comes that teasing lilt from my left.

I turn. "It was terrible."

She laughs, the sound unburdened and damn near joyful. "You're right. You were really bad. Comically so. It's sweet of your friends to try to make you feel better, though." She hikes her mat under her arm and glances back to where Goldie and Willa are chatting while Matty and Reid gather their animals and nestle them into matching carriers against their chests.

I swear, those two are something else.

"I'll see you tomorrow." Darcy tosses me a sweet smile, then steps away as the couples turn toward me.

Stay. The thought rises, unbidden and unwanted. I clear my throat but find I'm unable to say anything in response. All I can do is watch her sashay to her car, her body a fucking siren that will surely lead me to trouble if I choose to follow.

"Wanna walk the pier with us?"

I turn my attention to Matty and give him a short, "No."

They all laugh. "Told you he'd refuse," Goldie says, but her expression is kind. "It's a miracle you got Anthony to yoga. Take the win, guys."

She's right, but I don't bother speaking.

"Think you'll come back?" Reid asks. "Saw you talking to Darcy."

"Probably not," I answer, then start backing away, desperate to keep any conversation about Darcy from happening.

Matty comes to my rescue. "Leave the man alone, Officer Reid. You're a menace and a gossip of the highest order, and you know it."

"He's worse than Ox," I chime in, "and my brother used to be the biggest gossip in this entire town."

"No one beats Tom and Jerry," Willa says with a shake of her head. "Those two get all the hot gossip and feed it to Reid here. It's a vicious cycle."

I don't bother telling them that I probably know more than all of them combined. Bartenders hear far more than most people intend for them to, especially when alcohol loosens their tongues.

I turn away, letting my silence communicate everything it needs. They know I'm leaving, and they all know I'm not going to make a big fuss over it.

Back at the building, I still have hours to go before the place opens for the shortened Sunday hours. I feel…itchy. But I can't go for a run or work out; I've done plenty of that with yoga in the last hour. Only one other place that can cure me when I feel like this.

A short drive later, I'm making my way along through the overgrown path that leads to a secluded part of the beach. It's still on public property, but it's situated between two private sections so perfectly that most people don't realize it's here. And that's precisely why I love it: no people. I can swim or sit and contemplate the ocean without being bothered.

As I crest the small dunes and break through the grass, my feet sink instantly into the sugary white sand. I already feel better. With a deep breath, I start the short trek to my favorite spot on this stretch of beach and immediately see that someone is there.

I halt, then shake my head. This must be a cosmic joke. Because that someone is Darcy.

CHAPTER 7

DARCY

I S THIS EVEN happening right now? Anthony Hall is coming toward me, all six-feet-whatever growly of him, a pair of classic Wayfarer sunglasses donned casually as you please. Tattoos allll on display thanks to the tank top he wears, with short athletic shorts complete the jaw-dropping look.

Also: he was at yoga. The man has never gone, and today he goes?

Unfair.

Yesterday was bad enough, being forced to work alongside him and realizing just how fun he is to be around. Now this? How much more does the universe think I can take?

Resigned, I shade my eyes and watch him make his way across the powdery sand, his powerful legs flexing and damn near glinting in the sun. There's no point in not looking. Why deprive myself?

He pulls up next to me and sits, not bothering with any sort of towel. The scent of his beard oil catches on the breeze, warm and woodsy, along with sweat, and maybe a hint of bourbon from bartending. I don't bother talking; if I've learned anything with the man, it's that he'll speak when he's ready and not a moment sooner.

It takes him two minutes. Two minutes that feel like two hours. Two minutes to keep my anxious mouth shut. Two minutes in which I try, and fail, to keep my heart rate under control as I stare fixedly at the ocean. He shifts to face me, his eyes still shaded behind the Wayfarers. "How do you know about my secret spot?"

The question is jarring, and there's no keeping the shock out of my voice as I say, "Are you serious? It's *my* secret spot!"

His lips turn up the tiniest bit, and I have a feeling he's amused. Still, not another word.

Ugh. If that's how he's going to be, fine. I won't speak, either. I come here for the quiet and peace it brings, and dammit, Anthony Hall is not going to ruin that for me.

But…it's difficult. If someone is around, I want to talk to them. To fill the silence. So I try. I try really, really hard not to speak, digging twin divots into the sand with my feet as the minutes go by.

"Why are you so quiet?" he finally asks.

Oh, thank God. The words come out in a rush, as though a boulder had been lifted off my chest and oxygen was finally flowing back into my lungs. "I was trying to be quiet for you—I know I'm a lot; people tell me that enough so I guess it's true—but it was a special kind of torture, I'm not going to lie."

"Don't do that." He issues the directive to the ocean.

"Do what?"

"Change yourself. Not for me, not for *anyone*, but sure as hell not for me."

I open my mouth, but the man has rendered me mute.

He snorts. "At least this time you're quiet because I shut you up."

I'd let you shut me up any time you want.

The thought blooms, and heat stings my cheeks.

He notices, because his lips twitch faintly beneath his beard.

I refuse to let him have the upper hand, so I launch. "It'll be busy tomorrow. Some guys are coming to measure for the paneling, which will be attached to the ceiling and secured on the floor. I've got some great ideas about the colors…" I keep going, filling the silence space with details I'm certain I've already gone over with him, but I can't help it.

He reaches his hand out and touches my knee, and I stop talking. It's a tap, a tiny whiff of contact, but it's enough to send my blood boiling. Then he pulls his knees up and rests his arms on them, lowering his head to the cradle of his forearms. Greedily, I stare at the riot of colorful tattoos, using the time to catalogue how the cords of his muscles ripple with every twist of his wrist, the dark hair that dusts his arms and even his hands. "Sorry."

I didn't hear him correctly. "What?"

He takes a deep breath. "I shouldn't have touched you. I'm sorry."

Oh, if he only knew. "Why?"

He lifts his head to me.

"Will you please take the sunglasses off?" I can't take it anymore.

Wordlessly, he pulls them off. And I nearly pass out.

I don't think I've ever seen Anthony so unguarded. His hazel irises are like stained glass, flecks of gold nestled into sea green and surrounded by a band of navy. They are the most beautiful eyes I've ever had the pleasure of beholding, and it feels like the more I stare, the more he seems to see into me, as well.

Clearing my throat, I manage, "Don't apologize for touching me. Ever." Using his phrasing is all I can think to do.

He blinks, tearing his gaze from me in the process. I want his focus back on me so badly that I whine.

He whips his head back to me, clocking the tiny mewl that I let escape. But he says nothing, just stares.

I stare back. I see no point in hiding my interest anymore. Surely he knows I'm interested. How could he not?

His jaw ticks beneath his beard, and I'm overcome with the desire to touch it. I want to feel the roughness of it under my palm, over my mouth, between my legs. I want his hands cupping my breasts and hauling me onto his lap.

Basically, I *want*.

And it's that very want that has me unsure of how to behave.

"I won't apologize again if you won't," he finally says, blinking his attention back to the ocean in front of us.

Even the man's profile is striking. He is so entirely unfair that I want to kick my feet and shake my fist in protest. Believe me, the temptation is *high*. Instead, I lean back on my palms and give my attention to the waves before us. I lose myself in the steadying, soothing rhythm of its continuity, the absolute unstoppable nature of it. I think that's why I love coming here so much: because no matter what kind of mood I'm in, the ocean never wavers. Its colors might change, but that's only because of the sky above it.

Anthony reclines on his elbows beside me, his sunglasses back in place and safely hiding those perceptive eyes once more. And thank God for it. I've never felt so…*seen* as when he looked at me. As though the more vulnerable he let himself be, the more he saw of me in the process.

How in the fuck is that even fair?

Also not fair: his legs. Free of ink and thick with muscle, stretching out before us, tanned from a life of living at the shore. Beside him, my own legs aren't remotely similar, much more pale despite my frequent trips to the beach, and definitely less muscled. I'm strong, don't get me wrong, I have to be to do the kind of work I do, but I'll never have anything approaching definition in my thighs.

Which is fine by me. I like my body. It's strong, and healthy, and does everything I ask of it. I'll never be thin, but I've never really wanted to be. It seems a little boring, if I'm being honest. I enjoy standing out. I like wearing bright colors and putting my hair in bandanas and strutting around in tight skirts or overalls.

But back to the man beside me. The very confusing, but incredibly attractive, older man. The more I think about it, the more I find I care less and less about the age difference. Sure, he was seventeen when I was born. But I'm twenty-four now. Old enough to know precisely what I want.

The question is: does he want me?

Shaking my head at myself, I focus back on the serenity of the ocean, only for my stomach to growl at the lack of food it's been given today. Thankfully, Anthony doesn't seem to notice. Or if he does, he doesn't react. He seems just as lost in his thoughts as I am in mine.

I stand, turning away to brush the sand off and to shake the towel free. Someone has to leave, so I guess it's going to be me. Leaning to grab my Birkenstocks, I pause when Anthony pulls his sunglasses off to look at me.

"See you tomorrow?"

Why does it seem like that's a more loaded question than it should be?

"Yep. Bright and early," I chirp.

He nods, and without another word, I walk away. I don't look back, but I swear I feel his gaze on me.

Back home, I make an easy lunch of peanut butter and jelly sandwich and an apple, then head out to the garage. I know exactly what I'm going to do for the extra space in Anthony's loft. It finally hit me, and there's nothing to do but get started. Pulling out my notebook to start the sketch, I hope he likes it.

CHAPTER 8

ANTHONY

MID-JUNE. THE place is absolutely overrun with people, which is of course exactly how I like it. Kids dart in and out of the front area, strewing sticky fingers and sand in every direction. It'll be hell to clean, but that's okay—it's summer, and I expect no less than pure chaos. I'm behind the bar, same as most days, so I'm able to keep an eye on the more expensive aspects of things: the bar, the pool tables, and the bowling lane, all of which are packed in the post-dinner hour.

A few women around my age approach. They smile, their eyes tracking my every movement as I take their orders and start to make the drinks.

Harrison sidles up beside me, and in a low voice says, "The redhead is totally into you."

I shrug. "So?"

"*So*, you should go for it. I never see you sample the goods, boss." He grins and waggles his eyebrows for emphasis.

"No." And why is my answer immediately no? Because I still can't get a certain twenty-four-year-old out of my head. Seeing her on the beach last week was bad enough, but it's gotten worse. She's around nearly every day, wearing those damn overalls with a crop top beneath, revealing inches of skin that I'm desperate to taste, and it's torture. Pure and simple.

Would I like to forget all about her and bury myself in someone else? Yes. Will I? No.

Fuck.

I turn back to the much closer in age women and give them their drinks. Sure enough, the redhead flirts with me, her interest coming through loud and clear. And I don't respond, because nothing is going to happen. At all.

A few minutes later, exactly as I was anticipating, Darcy saunters in. She's freshly showered, her dark hair bound up in one of her signature bandanas, with yet another button-down that she's tied up over her navel, a pair of pants riding high and tight over her waist and hips. Guaranteed that when she turns around, her ass will be perfectly framed by the fabric, presenting it as though she gift-wrapped it especially for me. And I know she didn't dress for me, but tell that to my dick. Her siren-red lips part as she smiles.

"Mr. Hall. Fancy seeing you here."

I simply nod, not bothering to correct her anymore.

I take her in as she scans the bottles behind me. I know this game—the one where she absolutely knows what she wants to drink but makes me wait—and I love it. She gets to think she's annoying me, and I get to stare at her. Win-win. Before she can choose, though, Harrison appears, sliding his forearms onto the bar in front of her, smooth as fucking butter.

"Hey there, Darcy. Bowling league tonight?"

She nods, turning her gaze to him and smiling.

"Let me guess," he continues. "You want a Paloma. Nice and refreshing but still packs a punch. Just like you."

Darcy giggles. She fucking *giggles*, the sound sweet and bright, and now I'm going to have to kill Harrison. Or at least fire him. Because never in my entire time of knowing Darcy have I heard her giggle, and I hate Harrison down to his soul right now for being able to make her do it.

Asshole.

"That sounds great, Harrison. Thank you." Her eyes flit to me for the briefest of moments, and I'm certain she notes the fury in my expression. To her credit, she doesn't so much as flinch. But she doesn't keep her attention on me, either, turning to Amanda as she and Agatha appear, followed closely by Devon. I pull their drinks together, my attention utterly caught by the way Harrison keeps flirting with Darcy. And by the way she keeps letting him.

When he leans across the bar, stretching his hand to brush an escaped curl away from her face, I nearly lose my shit.

"Harrison," I bark.

With a shit-eating grin, he turns to me. "Yeah, boss?"

"Don't you need to get back to the front?"

He shoves his hands in his back pockets. "Sure do. Darcy, let me show you something really quick that I think you'll like." He rounds the bar and heads toward the front, where all the prizes and rental shoes are kept for the guests. And fuck me if Darcy doesn't follow him.

The other three women don't bother with any conversation with me, thank God. They make their way to the bowling lane closest to the bar, like always, and ready themselves for the practice session.

My blood is boiling.

Before I can do or say anything about it, Ox and Reid show up in street clothes.

"Hey, big bro!" Ox grins broadly. "Miss me?"

I grunt. Not even a little. But no way do I tell him that and hurt his feelings. Better to do what I always do and let him fill in the blanks.

Reid assesses me too quickly, as usual. "No. He didn't miss you at all."

Ox's face falls. "Why do you have to hurt me like that, Reid? Let a man have his dreams, will you?"

Naturally, *that* gets a smile out of me. "'Course I missed you, Ox." It's not the whole truth, but I'm unable to resist throwing Reid off the scent for once.

Ox grabs his chest and pouts. "You wound me, Anthony. Your lies are really something, you know that?"

Rolling my eyes, I pour the draft beer that Reid wants and look questioningly at Ox. He nods back, and I pour the same for him. Like Darcy, I never know what Ox will be in the mood for, so I can't ever just fill it without some kind of interaction. I'm sure it's how Ox wants it, the warm-hearted asshole.

"What are you up to?" I ask, sliding the beers across the bar.

"Figured we'd get a game of pool in, maybe check things out as civilians for once," Ox jokes. They tip their beers at me and head to the pool area. Of course, they know the locals, and within moments, they're racking up the balls with some of them.

Darcy comes back into my field of vision, my blood fizzing as I see Harrison trailing behind her with a pair of bowling shoes. Bowling shoes that I happen to know she does *not* need.

"Harrison!"

He startles, nearly dropping the shoes. "Boss?"

I narrow my eyes at him. He gets it without me having to say more, and in seconds he's hustling to set the shoes down and is back in front of the bar.

"What's up?"

"There's an entire store full of customers. You don't need to spend twenty minutes with just one."

Harrison grins mischievously. "You got something against Darcy, boss? Or just *me* with Darcy?"

I growl at him. There's nothing more to do.

And after I've refilled a couple of drinks for the women at the end of the bar, I whip my phone out and send a text.

He's not good enough for you

DARCY

Who's this?

You know who this is

DARCY

Ooh is Daddy mad?

I growl and shove my phone in my pocket. I have no business being in her business, and she definitely just reminded me of that. If she wants to let a boy flirt with her, then fine.

Chapter 9

Darcy

I'M EXHAUSTED. I'VE been busting my hump at Anthony's place, helping my dad at the hardware store a couple nights a week, and working on the surprise piece for Anthony's loft in the bit of spare time I have left. I'm bone-tired and need a day off. So even though it's a random Tuesday, I'm taking it. I live by the beach and haven't set foot on it since Anthony came and ruined my peace a few weeks ago.

Amanda answers my FaceTime almost immediately. "What's up, cutie?"

"Call off work today."

Her face lights up. "Are we playing hooky? Where are we going?"

"The beach. I'm pasty white and we need to remedy that, stat."

"I'm in."

"Perfect. See you soon. I'm gonna run by the shop and the Piggly Wiggly before I come get you."

"I'll be ready."

We click off and I throw on a two-piece and grab my beach

bag, already thinking of the snacks and sandwiches I'll pick up at the deli before grabbing Amanda.

But first: Dad.

His eyes widen when he sees me a little later, sunglasses propped on top of a messy bun and a raggedy T-shirt draped over my favorite pair of cut-off shorts. "What's wrong?"

I tilt my head. "What do you mean?"

"Did Anthony fire you? He's not called at all to complain, which I figured he would have done by now." His expression falls. "He did, didn't he? I'm so sorry."

I bristle. "Are you kidding me, Dad? Why would I have gotten fired when I'm doing an incredible job?" And I mean it, too: I'm kicking ass. I refuse to second-guess my talent. Life is too short, and I've had enough of that crap to last me a lifetime.

Dad's mouth opens and closes like a fish. "Well…then… what's all this about?" He waves his hand at my outfit.

"This is me taking a day off for my mental health," I shoot back. "Something even more necessary now that I know my own father doesn't have faith in me."

He has the decency to blush. "Sorry, Darcy girl. I look at you and still see you in pigtails, that's all. No matter how old you get."

"Maybe so, but your pigtail game was never that good, and this *little girl* is a grown-ass woman, Dad. You know it, and you need to treat me like it."

He lifts his chin, stubborn as always.

Wonder where I get it from.

I sigh, then round the counter to give him a hug. "Love you, you old coot."

"Love you too, girlie."

"Now where's that stack of invoices you said I needed to look at?"

I make quick work of the paperwork at Dad's, then pick up all the things at the Pig that we'll need to get through the day. I already know Amanda will have packed her own stash of goodies, and we'll have plenty. Which is the point. We stopped dividing up who would bring what years ago, because we never had enough when we did that. But when we leaned into the chaos of "just pack a bag," we discovered we always had plenty, and it was fun to see what we ended up with.

Finally, I pull up to Amanda's, and she gets in the car with her own beach bag stuffed to the gills. "I over-packed," she says.

Laughing, I aim towards the beach. "Good. Me, too."

There are a couple of good spots around, but we ultimately decide to head to the area just off the pier, where we can grab ice cream and rinse off before getting back in the car at the end of the day. It's definitely the more touristy part, and it's packed with mid-June tourists, but I don't mind. People-watching is one of my favorite things to do on the beach.

We unpack our bags, a little game of show and tell before settling into our routine of sunblock, sunglasses, and books. Combined, we have five peanut butter and jelly sandwiches, two giant bags of chips, a bowl of cut-up watermelon, a bag of baby carrots, strawberries that are on their last leg, and more water than we will possibly need. Also, sunscreen, two hats, and an extra pair of sunglasses. All in all, plenty to get us to dinner if we're so inclined.

I'm on my front, letting the sun soak into my back, when my phone goes off in my bag next to me.

"Who's rude enough to call when we're at the beach?" Amanda mumbles.

Reading the name on the screen, I laugh. "Anthony." Then I answer the FaceTime, not bothering with a hello because I know that'll irritate him—and honestly, irritating him is a lot of fun.

"Where are you?" His voice is gruff, sending a shiver through my body in delight. Then he squints. "Are you at the beach?"

"Your powers of observation are second to none, Mr. Hall," I deadpan. "What do you need?"

"Why aren't you here?"

I laugh. "Because I needed a day off. I've barely taken any time for myself, not that you've noticed."

"I notice when you're not here," comes the response.

The warmth that pools in my lower belly at his words should be concerning, but I don't say anything. I take a move from his own playbook and stay silent.

"You should have called, or texted," he grumbles.

"I didn't know I needed to tell you my every move, *Daddy*."

He growls, and I thrill to hear it. "I don't need to know your every move, Miss Belle, but as someone whose place you're working on, it's common courtesy to at least let me know that you won't be here. It's rude not to."

I sigh. "Fine. You might have a point." As much as I hate to admit it.

"I know I have a point."

Thankful for my sunglasses, I let myself stare at him. God, he's so sexy, especially when he's mad like this. There's a little line that furrows between his brows, and his hazel eyes sparkle with something that looks almost like worry. But why would he worry about me? Despite this call and the rare times I see him outside his normal routine, the man most often appears to simply tolerate me. I wish there were more to it, but I'm beginning to think I've made the rest up.

"Fine," I tell him. "I'm sorry for making you worry, Daddy."

His jaw ticks, but he doesn't bother to correct me on anything I just said.

Interesting.

"Are you going to be here tomorrow?"

I shrug, realizing that he's been getting a really impressive view of my cleavage this whole time. *You're welcome, Mr. Hall.* "Probably."

"Probably?" he repeats.

"Yeah, probably," I volley back. "Won't know till I wake up

and see how I feel. And quit giving me shit. You have no idea what I'm doing after I'm done at your place. It's not like I'm going home to eat bonbons." Whatever the fuck those are.

"What the fuck are bonbons?" he grouses.

I chuckle, because what are the odds? "I don't know. I've just heard the saying."

"Are you there with anyone else?"

"Seriously? It's literally none of your business." What the hell is it with the men in my life and their overprotective natures? I continue, "When have I ever given the impression that I need looking after, Anthony?" There's no disguising the way my voice tightens.

He must hear it, because he relents. "You're right. I'm sorry."

"Could you say that a little louder? I didn't hear you over the shock."

His lips curl infinitesimally, and the feeling is like being at the top hill of a roller coaster about to dive into the loop. "I'm sorry, Miss Belle. Better?"

I grin, the swoop of the fall sweeping through my body. *Miss Belle.* "Much."

"See you tomorrow?"

My grin widens. "Maybe." I click off before he can say anything else.

"Um, excuse me, but what in the banter was that and I need you to start explaining *immediately*." Beside me, Amanda pulls up into a seated position and unscrews the top of a water bottle.

"Eh, it's nothing." I sit up as well and open the container of watermelon. There is no better place than to eat watermelon than the beach, and I will stand on that hill.

Amanda pulls her glasses to the top of her head and pins me with her brown eyes. "Bullshit. You like him."

"I don't," I protest.

"Again: bullshit."

I shove a piece of watermelon in my mouth and use it as an excuse to keep quiet.

She raises an eyebrow, waiting, but I keep eating. In front of us, a group of guys around our age start a game of volleyball around the net they've spent far more time than necessary putting up. They're cute in that typical Alabama way: friendly faces, hair swooping just enough over their forehead that they've got to do that head-jerk thing to get it out of their eyes, and they probably all own multiple pairs of khaki shorts and tech polos with either University of Alabama or Auburn colors. Of course, they all have the usual blue patterns they consider to be their "nice" polos—they're the ones they'll wear to church when they peel themselves out of bed from drinking too much the night before.

And listen: no shade to them. Most of them have hearts of gold, and most of them can be trained on who to vote for and easily put in their place if they decide to try to be assholes to the women in their life. But as I look at them now, all I can think is... *no, thanks.*

Which is wild. I was never attracted to the vanilla guys anyway, but it's much more obvious now that I've spent time around Anthony. Anthony, with his full beard and Wayfarers. Anthony, with his tattoo sleeves and thick thighs and chest hair. And laugh lines around his eyes that probably aren't from laughing, which does something to my heart that I can't bear to think about. Anthony, who at seventeen years older than me, could probably fuck me at least ten different ways that I don't even have the imagination to think about.

"Um, hello?" Amanda waves her hand in front of my face. "Where did you go? Because you're staring at those guys and they're about to come over here and start flirting if you don't watch it."

I blink and look at her. "You'd eat those guys for lunch."

She throws her head back and cackles. "You're right. They can't handle all this."

All this is a thick body that won't quit, with tits and ass and belly and hips and legs that go for days—a fact that Amanda refuses to hide behind mounds of clothing. She's flawless and bold and usually has a line of men lined up to take her on dates and worship her afterward. She never keeps them around very long, though. Come to think of it, maybe *she* needs an older man.

"Damn right they can't," I confirm, then put the lid back on the remaining watermelon. "Time for more sunscreen? We can give those poor, unsuspecting boys a show."

"Definitely. Because that big guy is beyond hot, and I wouldn't mind a little more of his attention."

"Which one?"

"With the locs," she clarifies. "Looks like he played offensive line."

I dart a glance. He's the most interesting of the bunch, come to think of it. The sun glints off his dark skin, and the flirty smile he throws our way is cute. "As you wish," I say, reaching for the tube. "We going for the back first?"

She takes it from me. "Are you kidding? You're going to pretend to read while I rub it on my tits."

Laughing, I grab my book and resettle on the towel, preparing for the show Amanda's about to give them.

It works. Like a damn charm. And when the very guy she'd been targeting makes his way to us, eyes locked appreciatively on Amanda as he approaches, I can't help the little bit of jealousy at how easy she makes it. I'm never that uncomplicated. I never will be, though, and I guess there's nothing to do about that but lean into it.

CHAPTER 10

ANTHONY

I WAKE IN a sweat, chest heaving, dick straining. *This is ridiculous.* Yet another dream about Darcy. I was about to feel the dream version of what it would be like to sink into her, to hear her moan, to bury my face in her neck.

Throwing the covers off, I stalk to the bathroom and start a shower. Tempting though it is to turn on the cold and steep myself in it until my body gets the fuck under control, I do the opposite: hot. Hot as I can take it.

Ignoring my dick, which is still very much at attention thanks to the dream I was having, I lather up and wash, then rinse.

I should get out.

I should get off.

I'm not going to be able to focus if I don't do something about this. So, fuck it. Bracing one hand against the black and white tile, I take my aching cock in the other. The relief is instant, my eyes rolling back in my head as I think about Darcy. Her tits, way more than a handful, and the view I got on that call when she was at the beach...Her ice-blue eyes, challenging me, darkening with want when she thinks I'm not looking. That fucking *mouth*. What would it look like to fuck those red lips, to see her eyes water as I thrust into her mouth.

Fuck.

I grip harder, already close to the edge. Imagining her on her hands and knees, looking at me over her shoulder as I rubbed my hands over her perfect ass, hearing her beg for my cock. Making her beg more, before finally letting myself push into her tight pussy—

"Fuck! Fuck fuck fuck," I groan, spilling over my hand as I rest my forehead against the tile, not satisfied in the slightest but hoping I can at least focus.

I throw the water to cold, enduring it for all of two seconds before turning it off and stepping out. I make quick work of the rest, teeth, pits, contacts, then wrap the towel around my waist to step out.

Right into Darcy.

Who, judging by the wide eyes and flushed cheeks, might have heard me in there.

"Darcy."

In a blink, she's back to her usual self. "When are you going to learn to bring clothes to the bathroom, Mr. Hall?"

Fuck me if that doesn't sound better than ever coming out of her pert little mouth. "When are *you* going to learn to stop barging into my house without so much as knocking?"

She steps forward, crowding me with her watermelon-cherry scent. All I see are those glossy red lips and blue eyes, blinking up at me with ferocious indignation. "I knocked. You were too busy getting yourself off to hear me."

"You little brat." The words are out of my mouth before I can bite them back.

She raises a perfect eyebrow. "Tell me I'm wrong."

Fine. She wants to play? I close the space between us, noting with some satisfaction that she doesn't relent. *Good girl.* She inhales, her insane tits hitting my lower chest as she does. "No, Darcy. You weren't wrong."

Her lips tilt into a grin.

But I'm not done. It takes everything I have not to touch her as I say the next part. "And do you want to know who I was thinking of?"

She blinks.

"You. I was thinking of you, Darcy Belle. Taking my cock into my hands and imagining you. Thinking about bending you over my knee to teach you some lessons, and then, once your ass was nice and red from being spanked, I thought about laying you out on my bed and burying my tongue in your pussy."

Red stains her cheeks as her mouth opens, and she's breathing hard now.

If it's this easy to get a rise out of her with a few sentences—sentences that I made up to see if they'd get her going as much as they did me—I can only imagine what would happen if I let myself really go there with her. But that's not possible. I lean down and put my mouth next to her ear, making certain my lips hit the metal of the piercings running over the top of it. "The next time you come in my house uninvited, you'll be punished. Do you understand?"

"Yes." Her voice is rough. Raw. Needy.

I clench my hands, desperate to take her. To show her exactly what I mean. But I don't.

I walk away without another word, shutting myself in the bedroom that, thankfully, is now completely private and locked away from the rest of the space.

CHAPTER 11

DARCY

M Y BRAIN CAN'T seem to get the words to my mouth. My eyes can't seem to do anything but land on Anthony's ass as he walks to his bedroom and shuts the door.

And my mouth can't seem to close.

Anthony Hall wants me.

More than that, Anthony Hall wants to punish me.

The ache between my legs is nearly unbearable. I lower myself to the couch and squeeze my thighs, angling over the seam of my overalls for any sort of precious relief.

What am I going to do?

I'm going to do something, that's for damn sure. Because he finally gave me the tiniest glimpse of what's happening in that mind of his, and that taste was enough to leave me gasping.

Never mind listening to him in the bathroom. And for the record, I wasn't creeping on him. I came in and set my bags down, and it was impossible not to hear the way he was grunting and moaning in there.

And it was hot, okay? It was fucking hot as hell and even

though him being with another woman was definitely a possibility, I was drawn to the damn door like a moth to a flame.

Then I thought he might have actually said my name, which I'm sure was wishful thinking. I heard the water turn off, and I should have left. I know. But then I realized there was definitely not a woman in there, and before I could pull myself out of the fantasy of wondering what his ridiculous body might look like with water sluicing down it in the shower, the door opened and there he was, glaring down at me like it was my fault he had to get himself off in the shower.

And the things he said? Holy *shit*.

Never has it occurred to me that I might want to be punished, but now that he's said it, I…think I do.

I think I might be desperate for it, in fact.

But for now, I need to do my job.

Assuming I can actually focus.

With a groan, I leave the couch and make my way to the huge windows overlooking the ocean. What an incredible view. Who needs television when you have *this* to look at every day? The building faces northwest, and I bet this place gets a gorgeous sunset.

Maybe that's why he said he liked blues, greens, yellows, and oranges. It's the damn *sunset*. Grumpy, grunty, masculine as all get-out Anthony Hall loves sunsets. I know it like I know there are fish in the ocean.

Grinning, I turn to the day's work. I know exactly how to finish the pool table, for one thing. And now I know how to finish decorating.

If only I could finish myself. Ha.

Anthony emerges from the bedroom a few minutes later, dressed in his typical dark jeans and black Hall's Balls T-shirt, looking even more furious, if that's even possible. His boots stomp as he makes his way to the kitchen to brew coffee. I bite my lip at the noise coming from in there, the sound far more intense than it needs to be.

Good. He *should* be as frustrated as I am. I don't know why he didn't just kiss me. But I could have kissed him, too, so this is a two-way street.

I've just finished cutting in a perfect rectangle for the wiring in the drywall when Anthony's work boots appear in my periphery. I set my Dremel down and lift the safety glasses onto the top of my head, then sit back on my heels.

"Coffee." He thrusts it in my direction, and I note he's added the perfect amount of cream to it. I bet he's also added the precise amount of sugar that I like, too. Because make no mistake: I've noticed the appearance of both in his kitchen, and I know it's not for him. He takes his black, whereas I use mine as a delivery vehicle for delicious sugar and cream.

I take the mug and lift it to my lips, keeping my eyes on his the entire time. I'm more than aware of our positions here: him, standing before me, and me, kneeling in front of him.

I wonder how big his dick is. I bet it's big. *He's* big, so it only stands to reason that the man's dick would be proportionate. And, God, I bet he knows how to use it. The guys I've been with have been less than talented, and despite me directing them to angle this way and that, or go slower or faster, not one of them ever brought me to orgasm. Anthony, though? I bet he could make me come with ease.

"What's that look for?" he demands.

"Thinking how easily you could make me orgasm." If the man is going to talk to me about putting me over his knee and spanking me, then he better be prepared to get talked to right back.

His gaze narrows, but he doesn't speak.

Interesting.

"Anyway," I say, rising to my incredibly impressive five-feet-four, "thank you for the coffee. It's just how I like it."

He jerks his chin in a nod, then turns to leave.

"I'm grabbing lunch from the diner later. You want some?" We've done this before, so it's not a stretch for me to ask.

"No." He doesn't bother to look back at me, his muscles flexing beneath his shirt as he opens the door and slips out, shutting it behind him with a bang.

But you know what? Fuck that. I'm bringing him lunch, anyway.

A few hours later, my knees are aching from all the floor action I've done today, and I grip the railing to keep from buckling as I make my way downstairs. The sights and sounds of Hall's Balls are almost an assault after the calm solitude of the loft upstairs, and I plaster myself to the door, narrowly avoiding being run over by a very excited kid, waving handfuls of Skee-ball tickets as he runs to show them off.

Lights blink and flash all around me, kids squealing and hollering, the sound of balls cracking as a game of pool gets going. I actually remember coming here when it first opened. I was, what, fourteen? Yikes. Probably shouldn't be thinking of how my fourteen-year-old self used to come here to play pool and pretend I was grown up, because here I am now, working on the loft upstairs and wanting very much to bang the same man who was responsible for all that fun at fourteen.

With a glance in the bar's direction, I see the man himself braced against the bar, talking to a customer, his arms flexing as they hold him up.

I want to lick the divots in his arm muscles. That's how ridiculously distracted Anthony has gotten me—I'm thinking about divots in arm muscles, of all things.

But to be fair, there are no guys my age running around with divots in their arms. Maybe I'm looking in the wrong places for that, but yeah...I want the forty-one-year-old.

When I come back from the diner, I head to the bar without hesitation.

"Aw, did you bring me lunch, Darcy?" Harrison asks, flirting shamelessly with me like always. He's my age, maybe a few years older, and entirely appropriate for me. Maybe even legitimately interested. But I only have eyes for his grumpy boss.

Ignoring Harrison, I pull out the quinoa salad with extra chicken and dressing on the side and lay it in front of Anthony. It's his usual.

"I said I didn't want lunch."

"What makes you think I care what you do or don't want, Anthony?"

His eyes flash, the green in them blooming in irritation. What would it take to make his eyes *all* green? How furious would he have to be?

How bad is it that I want to see just how far I can push him?

Beside Anthony, Harrison watches us, his gaze bouncing back and forth as though we're the most interesting tennis match he's ever seen. Time seems to stretch, but I stay quiet, holding his gaze, letting the anger seep into me, swimming in it. Luxuriating in it. Wishing he'd punish me for not listening to him. Pissed off that he seems determined not to act on the attraction.

Finally, he grabs the to-go box and stalks to the other end of the bar, flipping the lid open and stabbing the food with a fork.

I win.

CHAPTER 12

ANTHONY

THE BOWLING LANES are on the fritz. I call Jim, like always, and he tells me to get Darcy to look at them.

"Jim, *you're* my bowling lane guy."

"Sure as shit couldn't tell you why," he shoots back. "I just get back there and poke around until something starts working. I'm telling you, Darcy is the better mechanic."

"Pretty sure Darcy is the better everything, Jim," I say, resigned.

Jim chuckles. "You're not wrong."

I click off and go upstairs, opening the door and bracing myself for the interaction. The place smells of sawdust and watermelon-cherry, and a song I don't recognize blasts into the air. Something kind of country, kind of rock and roll. Darcy's singing along, her back to me, swinging her lush hips. Her overalls are unhooked, held up only by the tool belt she wears, and her pink tank top rides up, revealing a thick strip of skin that I want nothing more than to nip and bite. I bet it's salty from the work she's doing.

It's been a week since she walked in and heard me. And while the promise of punishment has worked to keep her out of my space before 9 a.m., it's also unlocked every fantasy I could possibly have about her and then some. I'm jerking myself off every fucking day to thoughts of her, and sometimes twice. I need it to stop. Need her to be done with this damn renovation, but of course there have been delays with materials, and she's taken off more days this past week than ever before. But of course I can't ask her about them. Not after I sexually harassed her. I mean, she liked it, sure, and she gave it back to me just as good, but still. She's working for me.

She turns, and the glint of a navel piercing winks at me, and I think I might die. Jesus. A navel piercing in that soft stomach. Begging for me to trace it, to rub my head against her as though I'm marking her.

I am so very fucked.

She raises an eyebrow, then bends to turn the music off.

"Bowling lanes are on the fritz," I say. "Your dad said you were the one to talk to."

She preens. "Really? That was nice of him."

I shrug. "Nice or not, it's apparently the truth."

She sets the saw down. "It is, but he's never one to gush about me."

"I wouldn't say he gushed."

Her expression falls, and instantly I feel like an asshole. "Let me have my fantasy, Anthony." She stalks past me, her sweet scent trailing in her wake. "Well? You coming?"

I follow her down the stairs and into the hidden area behind the lanes. The fit is tight, of course it is, but Darcy ignores me completely, pulling a flashlight out of her tool belt and shining it around the mechanics. I lean against the far wall, staying out of her way as much as possible, and marvel at her.

She's focused entirely on the problem, her eyes flitting everywhere she shines the flashlight, and all it does is make me want her that much more. But it's more than that. Which is a problem.

Darcy makes a noise in the back of her throat, as though she's identified something, and turns back to me. "You didn't bring my tools?"

My lips part. "What?"

She gives a long-suffering sigh. "Anthony. If you're going to follow me around like an apprentice, then you have to act like one. I need my toolbox."

"I thought you had your tools right there." I point stupidly at the belt around her waist.

Reaching up to adjust the bandana around her head, she asks, "Do you really think I have what I need right here?"

She's definitely got what *I* need, so…maybe? I shake the thought away and mumble, "Be right back," before going to get the woman's tools.

A half hour later, I'm handing her whatever she needs as she demands it, watching as though I'm going to learn something and knowing good and well the only thing I'm learning is how luscious she looks with her ass bent into the air as she does something with a wrench. Which reminds me of yoga and the way she gave me such shit.

"I miss you," I blurt, then immediately regret it.

I blame her butt. I've been utterly transfixed by it, and suddenly I'm telling her I miss her.

She turns and straightens, slowly, as if fully aware she's the one in control right now. With her eyes pinned to mine, she says, "Good."

A laugh escapes me. "Good?"

Her plush velvet lips quirk up. "Yeah. Good. Because I like talking to you."

She emphasizes the word *talk* and I have no idea what to do with that. Is that code for something? Does everyone her age know what that means and I'm just an old fuddy-duddy with no clue of what "kids these days" do?

I am a disaster.

She must see the confusion on my face, because she laughs.

Then, with the softest smile I've ever seen on her face, she says, "I miss you, too."

I clear my throat. "As—as friends."

The smile falters and her eyes dim as she blinks, then nods once. "Right. As friends."

It's an asshole thing to do, and I know it. But I'm losing control here and the only way I know to take it back is to put some distance between us. I could feel myself wanting to kiss her. To do whatever I want to her. And I can't. She is too young. And I am...well, I'm not old, exactly, but I'm too old for her.

She finishes up quickly, the silence suddenly stilted and awkward, and I lead her back out. She takes her leave without another word, turning to the loft while I go back to my comfort zone behind the bar. It's the one place I control everything, and good God, do I need some fucking control right now.

I exhale, willing my thoughts to settle, needing to drop into the mindlessness of work.

But of course, this is the exact moment Ox chooses to waltz in, brandishing his phone screen at me as he closes the distance. "Okay, big brother, it's time."

"For what?" Then I see it's Levi on the screen and inwardly groan. This is about—

"Planning Mom and Dad's party and Dad's retirement!" Ox's smile is so big and bright that it damn near hurts my feelings.

"Anthony," Levi intones.

"Levi," I return. We don't talk much—okay, we don't talk at all—but I really wish the asshole lived here. Ox would be a hell of a lot more, I don't know, manageable. But Levi has a life in New Orleans with his wife, so whatever.

"I'm thinking we'll have it here." Ox dives right in.

"No." Levi and I speak simultaneously.

Ox's face falls. "Why not?"

"We can do better than that," Levi answers.

"Fuck you," I growl.

"Fuck you right back," Levi says. "You don't want to have it there anyway, so don't get your panties twisted. Your place isn't good for this, and you know it. We need a place that we can do up all fancy and shit. You know Mom would love that."

I fight the urge to slam the phone to the ground. Whether I want to have the party here or not is beside the point. But for Levi to say my place isn't good enough? Fuck him. Growing up, we would have all killed to come to a place like this.

Whatever. I'm not nearly as close to my parents as my brothers are. Which makes sense, I guess. I was six when they were born; old enough to fend for myself, and that's exactly what I had to do. Mom had her hands full with the twins, and Dad was either working, grading papers, or doing side jobs to try and make ends meet. And even once the boys got older, they still took all the attention. I was always quiet and watchful, and my brothers were most definitely not. These days, it's as though they're only proud of the twins, and I guess I get it—one's a successful lawyer and the other is the town chief of police. But it's not like I haven't done well for myself. I run a successful family entertainment venue off the pier. How is that not enough? They've been here all of one time.

I focus my attention back to the conversation that's continued without me.

"Can we pay someone to do the decorating?" Levi's asking.

"Where?"

Ox levels an exasperated look at me. "At the rec center, Anthony. Were you paying *any* attention or were you just being broody, like always?"

I don't answer. Because clearly, I was "being broody," even though I disagree with the way he couches it. Also, how is it that the rec center can be made "fancy," but my place can't?

Levi snorts. "Good old Anthony. Always consistent, brother. Never change."

The comment chafes. "We'll do it here."

"No," Levi responds. "I don't want little gremlins running around when we're trying to have a nice party for Mom and Dad."

"I can close the place."

"I'm with Levi on this one," Ox says. "The rec center makes more sense. Plus, they have a kitchen, and you don't. Which is wild, by the way. When are you going to fix that? The amount of money you could make on pizza alone—"

"Ox, focus," Levi snaps, his patience clearly wearing thin. "Anthony, can you find me someone to hire to decorate the rec center?"

I have no idea, but before I can say that, Levi bulldozes on.

"Ox, can you reach out to the caterer?"

"Of course."

"Then we're done here. Talk to you later."

The screen goes dark, and Ox looks up at me. "Guess we've got a plan."

Gritting my teeth, I answer. "Guess so."

"Tell me what's going on with Darcy."

Startled, I meet his eyes. For as goofy as my little brother may pretend to be, he is incredibly smart and observant as hell. It's what makes him such a great police chief. It's also what got me in trouble more times than I care to admit. "Nothing."

He tilts his head. "You really expect me to believe that?"

"I don't really care if you believe it or not. That's the truth."

He snorts, sounding exactly like his twin, and slides off the stool. "Okay. Keep telling yourself that. And let me know when you're ready to talk."

I watch him walk away, images of Darcy and her tool belt swirling in my head, unable to decide if there's really anything to talk about or not.

CHAPTER 13

DARCY

FOURTH OF JULY. And a beautiful day it's going to be. I make myself an iced coffee in my little cottage, spending the morning in solitude while I straighten up around the house, doing a couple of loads of laundry in the tiny washer and dryer stacked in the back, and packing my beach bag for a long day at the shore.

My eyes catch on my tool belt and bag in the kitchen. I can't believe I've been renovating Anthony's loft for nearly eight weeks. I've gotten a lot done, but because Anthony is a bit of a penny-pincher, it's only me doing the work. I pull my guys Kevin and Jeff in when needed, but that's been pretty rare, and only when I need some serious muscle. It's nearly finished, and it's absolutely gorgeous. I can't wait to see the finished product. The pool table is coming along too, although not as quickly as I'd prefer. It's my first one and the learning curve is slowing me down.

At ten, I pull up to Amanda's place and she runs out, her hair in braids on either side of her head and her favorite Fourth t-shirt on. "Nice shirt," I laugh, taking it in like the national treasure it is. There's an eagle on it, but it's sitting astride a unicorn. The unicorn has red, white and blue stripes coming out of its butt as it leaps across the Grand Canyon. Emblazoned across the top is the phrase: *The smell of freedom.* It's entirely hilarious, and I cackle every time she pulls it out.

"Thank you." She bows her head, then nods at me. "Not bad yourself."

I laugh. "It's a new one this year." It's much simpler than Amanda's, with George Washington in sunglasses against the flag and the words *It's only treason if you lose.*

"Perfection. Let's get this show on the road!"

I drive to the beach, which is absolutely packed, but we manage to find a spot. We get settled, and Amanda pulls out a fizzy alcoholic drink. "Want one?" she asks.

I shake my head. "Way too early."

She lowers her sunglasses and glares. "No such thing on the Fourth, missy."

I shrug and raise my bottle of water. "I'll be fine."

"Suit yourself." She pops the can open, pours it into her cup, and takes a sip. "Ah. Happy Fourth, Darcy!"

I chuckle. "Happy Fourth, Amanda."

"So is Daddy coming?" She waggles her eyebrows.

"My dad? Yeah, later."

She snorts as she crumples the can and buries it in her tote. "No, Darcy. *Daddy.* Anthony Hall."

My cheeks burn as I look for something else to do. "Oh."

She cackles now, pointing at my blush. "Yeah—*oh.* So, tell me how that's going along."

I groan and cover my face, my hands muffling my voice. "Absolutely nothing is going on."

"Still?"

"Still."

She sighs. "When is he going to stop being all uppity about it and bang you?"

I laugh. "It's not all about being banged." Even as I say it, the words surprise me. It's not?

"Sure it is. That man is fine as hell, and even though older men aren't my thing, we both know that he could do some serious damage to your uterus."

I pull my hair out of the elastic so I can re-twist it to the very top of my head. "I don't even know where to start with all that."

"Oh, shit. You like him, don't you?"

I hesitate. Do I? Oh no.

Amanda points at me. "Oh, my God. You *do*. It's more than just wanting to bang him, isn't it?"

I hang my head, realization slamming into me. "I'm so down bad for him, it's stupid."

Amanda pats my leg reassuringly. "Then I think you need to go after him, my love."

"I don't think he wants me."

"After everything you've told me, how could he not? Of course he does. You just have to convince him that the age thing isn't a big deal."

"I'm pretty sure I can get him to sleep with me—that's not the problem."

"Then make it happen!"

Shaking my head, I twist and untwist the cap of my water bottle. "I want more than that, Amanda. I think. I don't know." I groan. "What if he's so good at it that I get addicted?"

"You should be so lucky," Amanda says with a laugh, rolling her eyes. "Now excuse me while I go flirt with the easy, uncomplicated boys over there." She stands, then sashays over to where some guys around our age have set up a tent.

In moments, she's got the invite for us to join them, and I do. There's no reason that my angst over Anthony should stop my friend from getting her flirt on.

"Hey, gorgeous," one of them says. He's wearing an Auburn hat turned backwards, his bare chest golden and taut. He wears a gold chain around his neck, and his grin would normally devastate me with how hot it is.

"What's your name?" I ask him.

"Derrick," he answers.

I smile. "Derrick. You're cute."

His grin widens as he swaggers closer. "So are you."

I step back and hold a hand up. "And I'm not interested."

He quirks a brow. "You sure?"

"Roll Tide, Derrick," I deadpan, letting him know with that one phrase that my loyalty is with the University of Alabama and not Auburn.

He laughs good-naturedly. "Ugh, *fine*. But you're going to let me get you a drink, yeah?"

"Sure thing."

We spend the next hour with the boys, and Amanda flirts her ass off. She has a great time and gets far more drunk than she needs to be so early in the day. I drag her to the ocean for a quick cool-off, and when we're done, we head back to our own towels and dig into lunch.

After a while, my dad shows up, and so do Agatha and her daughter Betty. Soon after that, Devon trudges through the sand towards us, with Aaron close behind her in navy blue paramedic gear.

I hug Devon, then ask her husband, "You on duty?"

Aaron nods. "Yeah. The beach and booze never go well together. Add in all these people, and something's bound to happen. But I wanted to come say hi, see how everyone is before getting back to it." He nods toward the street, and I see the bright red paramedic golf cart, tricked out with wheels for the beach, with another guy sitting in it. He waves, and I wave back.

Devon leans in. "You know, he's single."

Aaron laughs. "Don't try to pimp Sam out. I have a feeling that Darcy would scare him."

"Why, because he can't handle a carpenter?" I shoot at him.

"Because he can't handle someone as self-assured as you," Aaron corrects. "He's still young and stupid."

"He's the same age as Darcy!" Devon protests.

"Exactly," Aaron says. "She isn't interested."

I hold my hand up for a high-five. "Damn, Aaron, you're good."

He winks. "I know a thing or two." And his expression makes me think he may know way more than I realize.

He gives his wife a kiss and takes off.

"So," Devon says, her eyes well and truly on Aaron's ass as he walks away, "are we really going to do this tournament in a few months?"

"It's four months away. We can totally do it," I pronounce. "Sure, we need to practice—"

"We need a miracle," Agatha interrupts.

"Fine, we might need a miracle. But so what? It's fun, right?"

"I'm not doing this for bowling glory," Amanda agrees. "It's fun. It'd be more fun if guys our age participated, but whatever. I like hanging out once a week."

"Definitely a highlight," Devon agrees.

"I've had better," Agatha jokes. "But miracle or not, we'll do it."

Dad pops his head into the conversation. "I, for one, think it's really neat what you girls are doing."

I chuckle. "Neat?"

His cheeks tinge pink. "Leave me alone, Darcy girl. I said it's neat—what's wrong with that?"

"Not a thing," I say. "In fact, you're adorable."

He laughs self-consciously and shoots a sidelong glance at Betty. "Thanks."

I make myself ignore what that look at Betty might have meant, because that would mean Dad might actually be interested in someone. And while I can't hold that against him at all, I *can* totally ignore it because it's gross.

I never want to think about my dad even so much as kissing someone. Does that make me a ten-year-old? Probably.

It's probably five o'clock by the time I realize Amanda is utterly and completely obliterated. We've spent hours in the sun, with folks rotating up to grab hot dogs and sodas, and without realizing it, I've allowed Amanda to drink all her beverages plus mine. I just wasn't feeling it today, but clearly, Amanda was.

Devon looks at me over her sunglasses. "Pretty sure it's time to get our girl here out of the sun." She stands and gestures to Amanda, who is about to fall asleep under the umbrella that Betty and Agatha brought with them.

I stand and brush the sand off, shoving my legs into my jean shorts and sliding my feet into the softened beach flops I've had for literally a decade. "I've got her," I wave Devon off.

"You sure?" Devon gives me a dubious look. "I'm sure you can handle her, but she's…" she laughs. "Absolutely wasted."

I chuckle. "It's okay. We're all allowed to get a little twisted sometimes. She's safe with me." I finish packing all our stuff and lean over to her, nudging her awake. "Hey, sleeping beauty. Let's get you home."

Amanda turns a bleary eye on me. "You sure? I thought we'd stay for the fireworks."

"No way will you make it to the fireworks, my love," I giggle. "Come on. I'll get you home and tucked into bed."

It takes double the time to get to my car as it did to get onto the beach, but half of that is because there are even more people than there were before. Soon enough, I've got her buckled up and we're heading to her house, the windows down and no sound but the wind coming through the open windows.

Another half hour and I've gotten her through the shower and tucked into bed, a bottle of water and two Ibuprofen on her bedside table for whenever she wakes up.

I check my watch. I don't really want to go home, and I'm not feeling heading back to the over-crowded beach for the fireworks. Which, of course, means I'm heading to my secret beach.

Traffic is bonkers, with more people streaming into the area to see the fireworks. And I don't blame them—I've not missed the fireworks in twenty-four years and I'm not going to now.

I finally find a place to park and begin the walk to my sanctuary. As I crest the dunes and look down, it's easy to see just how high the tide has gotten. The sun has already disappeared, and the sky is steadily turning purple, with streaks of orange and pink streaking through. I exhale, relishing the comforting familiarity of where I am, the beauty of the sunset. Ahead of me, a shadowy figure sits on the thin strip of beach, their back to me and angled towards the spot where the fireworks will go off.

I don't want to startle them, so I call out as I get closer. "Hey! Sorry—I'm just gonna—"

The words die on my mouth as the figure turns. It's Anthony.

Because of course it is.

CHAPTER 14

ANTHONY

THIS HAS TO be another cosmic joke. Because there is no way in hell that the very woman who's ruining my life is coming my way in the dusk, hips swaying far too deliciously against the backdrop of sand, lips turned up as if she's in on the joke and knows I'm at the end of my rope.

Swallowing and standing, I give her what I hope is a friendly smile. "Darcy Belle. To what do I owe the pleasure?"

Her smile widens, and the joy on her face is the sweetest hit to my solar plexus. "Anthony Hall. To what do *I* owe the pleasure? Shouldn't you be manning your fine establishment?" I don't miss the way she scans me head to toe, and I've never been more grateful to be shirtless.

I shake my head. "Nah. Harrison always takes over for the Fourth. He doesn't like the fireworks, and I love them, so..."

"Harrison is afraid of fireworks?" The gleam in her eye is positively endearing as she closes the space between us.

"I didn't say that," I hedge.

"But you didn't *not* say that," she fires back.

All I can do is shrug and smile.

"There you are," she murmurs.

I frown.

She laughs. "No, don't do that!" Setting her tote down and sliding off her flip-flops, she laughs more. "I finally see one of those rare smiles and then you instantly frown!"

Naturally, my frown deepens.

She giggles, then undoes her shorts and drops them to the sand before pulling her shirt off.

My mouth dries. She's wearing a retro-style two-piece, bright red with stripes, her curves on display more than any time I've seen before, and it takes everything I have not to pull her to me. When I lift my gaze back to her face, she smirks, and I know I've been caught.

She laughs quietly, turning to walk the few feet to the surf. "Ah, Anthony—you're the *worst!*"

Somehow, I don't think she means that. After a moment's hesitation, I take a step toward her.

She leans down and makes to splash some water at me. I flinch and jump back, and it only serves to make her laugh harder.

"Let me guess—Harrison is afraid of fireworks, but *you're* afraid of the ocean?" she teases.

I cross my arms. "I am no such thing."

Raising a dubious eyebrow in the fading light, she splashes me again.

"That's it," I growl, reaching out to grab her.

She squeals and leaps away, her movements hampered by the heavy surf lapping at her thighs. Then she turns and splashes again, but the waves catch her off-guard and she pitches forward.

I lunge, catching her in my arms and pulling her upright just as the wave crashes into my knees.

"Shit, how did we get this far in?" she laughs, breathless.

"Probably because you weren't paying attention," I admonish, a smile playing on my lips.

Her eyes zoom to my mouth and lock there, heating as I lick

the salty water away. Then, without warning, she steps away and heaves a handful of water at me.

"You little brat," I call out as she yelps and ducks out of my reach, trying like hell to outrun me.

She's got no chance. I catch up in two strides and haul her to my chest, picking her up and holding her out of the water against my chest, one arm tucked beneath her legs and the other cradling her back.

"Put me down!" she commands, her voice high-pitched with laughter.

"Are you sure about that?" I ask, taking us a little farther in. "If I put you down, you're getting dunked."

Her eyes shimmer with delight as she tightens her grip on me. She doesn't speak.

It dawns on me that I have her in my arms. All of her. My breath is hot and fast with the realization, and God, does she feel amazing. Her curves plastered against mine, her nipples pressed against my chest. She relaxes into the hold, not seeming the least concerned that I'll drop her, and something inside me cracks wide open.

Above us, the sound of the first firework crackles above us, and the colors reflect in her eyes. Darcy's lips tilt into a pleased smile, her gaze on the sky.

"Do you trust me?" I don't recognize the gruffness in my voice.

She looks back at me. "Always."

Without another word, I turn us to shore, striding through the surf and aiming for the towel I'd laid out earlier. She holds on as I move, her eyes darting over my face, shoulders, and chest before resting again on my lips. I can't explain how I know the path her gaze takes since I'm not watching her; I simply do.

Maybe it's because that's the very same path my own eyes have traveled a million times, wondering how her skin would taste. How her lips would feel beneath mine, soft and pliant.

I kneel in the sand and lay her on the towel, lowering myself beside her, refusing to miss a second of watching the droplets of water trail from her forehead down to her temples.

The fireworks shoot off above us, and still, she keeps her eyes on me. "Anthony." My name on her lips is something like a plea, and I finally can't refuse her. Not anymore.

With my finger, I trace her temple and soft cheek, positioning her exactly where I want her. Then I lower my mouth to hers.

She tastes like she smells: watermelon and cherry, with a little sea salt thrown in. I hold there, reveling in the feel of them, knowing it's the only time I'll feel them for the first time, and desperately wanting to bottle the moment forever.

Darcy's lips open and mine follow, desiring to give her exactly what she wants. What *I* want. And as the fireworks boom above us, I slide my tongue into her mouth, exploring, tasting, nipping and sucking. She moans and sighs beneath me, threading one hand into the hair at the nape of my neck while the other cups my face, feeling my beard before sliding down to my chest.

Kissing her is everything I thought it would be. By turns innocent and chaste, then lush and lewd. When I pull away to look at her, she grins back softly, her eyes gentle even as they're blown with lust.

"More," she whispers. "Kiss me again, Anthony."

I groan. I couldn't resist her request if I tried. Lowering my lips to hers once more, I slant my mouth and take hers with an ownership I probably shouldn't feel. There's no stopping the way I want to possess her. To claim her as mine for all the world to see. I release her lips, kissing a trail down her chin to her neck, breathing in the overwhelming scent of her as I nibble the skin beneath her ear and feel her shiver beneath me.

"Cold?"

"No," she sighs. "You found the spot that makes me crazy, that's all." Her arms tighten around me, her nails raking down my chest.

Hissing in surprised pleasure, I nibble once more, relishing the feel of her squirming in my arms.

I move back to her lips, plunging my tongue into her mouth with abandon. I want her. Want to feel the tightness of her wrap around my dick and hear her breaths quicken as she nears release.

When her hand dips down my stomach, angling to slip into my shorts, I almost let her. Instead, I put my hand on her wrist, halting its path.

"Because you don't want to?" she asks, her eyes searching mine with obvious vulnerability.

"Does it feel like I don't want to?" I ask, guiding her hand to my dick.

Her eyes flash, then heat once more. "So why not?"

"Because the first time we do anything, it's not going to be on the beach like a pair of horny teenagers."

She rises, pushing me onto my back and shifting to push me onto my back. I go willingly, taking in the way her lush curves are silhouetted by the fireworks behind her as she straddles me. Her thighs grip my hips, and her center is warm and damp, and I groan again, knowing the dampness isn't because we've been in the ocean. "Darcy."

Biting her lip as her eyes roll in the back of her head, her hips swivel slowly on top of me as she seeks her pleasure. Tendrils of wet, dark hair fall from the bun on top of her head, framing her beautifully as she moans. "God, Anthony. Say it again. Say my name again."

"Darcy." My voice is gravel as I wrap my hands around her thighs and grip so hard I'm certain they'll leave bruises. "I want you. I want you in so many ways that it'll take me years to be satisfied, and even then, it'll never be enough."

"Fuck, Anthony." She moves a little faster.

"Am I getting you off, baby girl? Is my filthy mouth all it takes?" I watch her greedily, clocking every nuance of her expression, the way her mouth opens, the flush I shouldn't be able to see in the dark but swear I can anyway, the hardness of her nipples that I'm keeping my hands off by willpower I didn't think I possessed.

She whimpers. "I think so."

I take over the rhythm, my dick so fucking hard that I might explode. "Ride my cock, baby. Get yourself off. I want to see you come. I want to know what you're gonna look like when I'm fucking you."

She pants, falling onto my chest with her hands, her nails digging half-moon crescents into my chest. It feels perfect. *She* is perfect, lit by fireworks from above.

"There you go," I murmur, my voice going as deep as it can. "You're almost there, aren't you? Come for me."

"Fuck," she breathes. "Holy fuck." Her hips buck, taking what she wants from me, and she whimpers as her entire body shudders, head thrown back and eyes closed tight with the orgasm.

I watch in rapt fascination, both devastated and wholly obsessed.

This woman will be my ruin. Everything about her was tailor-made to torture me, and all I want is more. So much more.

Her breath coming in soft gasps, Darcy opens her eyes and finds mine.

My lips tip up. "That was the sexiest thing I've ever seen in my life."

She smiles, her eyes hazy with pleasure. "That was the sexiest thing I've ever experienced in my life. So, we're even, maybe?"

I chuckle, shifting and rolling us so that she's on her back and I'm between her incredible legs. "It's not about being even. Never."

She blinks. "That's...not what I'm used to."

The words are a cold splash of reality, and my dick gets the memo as well. This shouldn't be happening. Yes, she's an adult, but she's had such little life beyond this. I don't think she even went to college. I've got almost two decades on her. There's a big difference. Though I'm not sure she cares.

"Where'd you go, Daddy?"

I jerk back to reality to find her grinning saucily at me. "You and that Daddy word," I grumble.

"Tell me you don't like it."

Biting the inside of my cheek, I admit, "Not sure I can say that, Darcy."

She shivers even as she beams. "Thought so."

I frown. "You're cold."

She tries to protest, but I stand and pull her up. "Let's get you to your car so you can warm up."

She laughs. "Anthony, it's easily eighty-five degrees. I'll be fine."

"Maybe, but the fireworks are over, anyway."

She glances up at the sky, her lips swollen, her dark hair gloriously disheveled. "Fine. Walk me to my car?"

I hear the question in her voice, but I ignore it. We went too far as it is. I don't want her regretting anything.

We get ready, pulling on clothes and packing away the towel, before she digs in her bag for a flashlight. It's dim, but it's all we need to see our way through the dunes and back to the street.

When we get to her beat-up Camry, she pops the trunk and digs into yet another tote, producing dry clothes.

She looks at me, bemused. "What? You don't have a change of clothes in your trunk?"

"Of course not."

"Anthony, we live at the beach. It's summer. How do you *not* have a change of clothes in your trunk?"

"Because I'm forty-one," I answer.

She rolls her eyes. "Your age has nothing to do with it." After a beat, she glances down at my crotch and back. "Clearly."

I chuckle. "Okay, you. How are you changing your clothes?"

"In my back seat," she says, winking at me. "You wanna stand guard?"

After a few minutes—minutes in which I behave myself and don't stare at her while she's in various stages of undress—she emerges in a fresh T-shirt and shorts. No bra.

My mouth instantly waters. "Darcy."

She shakes from side to side, sending her luscious breasts bouncing and swinging. "You like?"

I wipe a hand down my face. What I'd give to have those tits around my face. "I'm trying really hard to be good here."

She presses herself against me, soft and warm. "I'm trying really hard to understand why."

Me, too. I take in her upturned, sunburned nose and see the beginnings of beard burn forming around her mouth. I can't help the smirk that forms, knowing that anyone who sees her tomorrow will know she's been up to something.

"Be good," I admonish, popping a kiss onto her forehead and walking away before anything else can happen.

Chapter 15

Darcy

PLEASE EXPLAIN TO me why I've spent the entire weekend *not* chasing after Mr. Hall like a woman obsessed. I should, right? The man let me ride him like a fucking horse until I came, for God's sake. But I didn't. Instead of attempting to glue myself to his side like a barnacle, I spent Saturday at the hardware store, sorting through what felt like a billion pounds of paperwork and showing Dad, yet again, how to use the accounting software. I swear, the man's learned incompetence is going to send me to an early grave.

"You're better at it," he'd protested.

"Yeah, well, it's your store, Dad," I reminded him.

I extracted what felt like a blood oath from him to do better, and by Sunday, I was exhausted. The thought of seeing Anthony at yoga was almost enough to get me to go, but something told me his appearance might have been a onetime thing, anyway.

By the time Monday morning rolls around, I've decided I need the coldest, frothiest coffee around, along with a chocolate croissant, to really get my day started off right. With a smirk, I pull out my phone and type a message to Anthony.

> I'll be a little late to the loft, Daddy. Grabbing some coffee.

The message immediately shows as read, but he doesn't respond, which makes me laugh. Because of course he doesn't.

I'm waiting in the line for my coffee when someone calls my name. I turn, and it's my ex. "Jason."

He smiles, and his eyes take a leisurely stroll over my body like they have a right to. It makes my skin crawl. We ended things on good terms, but I'm not a fan of being looked at as though I exist purely for a man's gaze.

Surprising no one, really.

"Eyes up here," I snap.

His grin gets broader. "Sassy as always," he chuckles. "How are you?"

I don't bother answering. Somehow, having the word *sassy* be a descriptor of me come out of his mouth is yet another thing I don't like. Still, the guy's around town, and this isn't exactly a booming metropolis. Shoving down the urge to tell him to keep his eyes and mouth shut, I aim for common ground. "You still at the library?"

He nods, standing straighter, and when he speaks, there's a tinge of…whining, almost? "Of course. I'd be head librarian if it weren't for old Mr. Stringer."

I force my face to remain neutral, and boy howdy, is it hard. I fucking *love* Mr. Stringer. He was single-handedly responsible for my love of reading, not that I have much time to do it right now. He'd realized early on that I wasn't the fluffy book kind of girl and immediately had me flying through action and adventure books, then murder mysteries and spy stories. It's entirely possible I wasn't old enough for some of the novels he gave me, but what's wrong with reading about a dead body now and then?

"He's still there, huh?" I say instead.

Jason's face pinches. "Says he's got another few years in him."

He straightens one arm and adjusts the fit of his button-down, far too starchy for the humidity of the day outside. "Anyway." He pauses and takes a breath, seeming to steel himself for the next part. "Would you, ah, be interested in maybe meeting for coffee or something?"

I bark out a laugh. "No." There isn't even a remote possibility I'm interested in this man. He's nothing I want, and all this conversation is doing is proving that he has some serious work to do on himself. Even if he did, someone like him would never satisfy me. For that matter, Jason never satisfied me, anyway. Seems I'm destined to want a broody, grumpy bartender instead.

Jason looks shocked. "Really? I thought—"

"Darcy!" The barista calls my name, and I turn without another word to grab my drink and croissant.

"Yeah, like I said—no thanks." And because I can't help myself, I look him straight in the eye as I take a giant slurp of my drink, then close the distance between us to give him a conde-scending pat on the head as I leave. "Good luck."

Not gonna lie, the whole interaction puts a little pep in my step.

I'm late enough that Anthony is already downstairs, his back to me as I let myself in, the open door sending a streak of early-morning sun into the dimly lit arcade. He shifts, looking my way, but he's far enough away that I can't tell what his expression is.

"Good morning," I call out.

He nods, a simple jerk of his head, and says nothing.

Standard. It's standard behavior and yet it irritates the crap out of me. The man dug his fingers into my thighs so hard they left little bruises, and all he does is jerk his head down in a silent hello.

Ugh. Whatever. I'm still in a good mood and he can't take that from me. With another hearty slug of my coffee, I head upstairs and get to work.

Lunch comes and goes, and no sign of Anthony. I eat my

peanut butter and jelly sandwich, not happy about the lack of the man, but also fully aware that we're in the thick of summer. He's probably dealing with shrieking kids and exasperated moms—a combination so heinous that I frankly have no idea how he deals with it.

A little before four, I've done as much I'm going to do and flop onto the couch I have plans to replace. At four on the dot, the door opens.

I rise from the couch and stare at him.

He stares back.

"Where have you been?"

His brow furrows. "Working." He strides to the kitchen and pulls a jug of water out of the fridge, pouring some in a fresh glass and looking up at me with a question in his eyes as I enter. When I shake my head, he puts the water back in the fridge and picks up his glass, downing the liquid in a few gulps.

I watch him, silent, and wonder how is it that even his Adam's apple is sexy. Suddenly, even him drinking water is enough to get me going.

"Where were you?" He pins me with an unreadable expression.

"Working," I shoot back. "Where else would I have been?" *This game sucks.* I push off the door—which is trimmed beautifully, I might add—and close the distance to him.

He evades me, shifting past and leaving the kitchen to go back into the bigger space. I swear I hear him chuckle as he does it, but that's probably because of the growl that issues from my throat.

"Anthony." I follow him. No way does he get to ignore me.

He turns, crossing his arms in front of his chest. "Darcy."

Heat spears through me at the way he says my name. It's part warning, part desire, and one hundred percent my undoing. So. Fuck it. I'm laying my cards on the table. "I want you. Maybe the women you're used to aren't this straightforward—"

He huffs, the faintest grin tipping his lips. "Oh, trust me. There is no one on earth like you, Darcy."

Heat warms my chest at the praise, whether he intended it or not. "I want this. Whatever this is," I gesture between us, "I want it."

His eyes shutter. "You don't. What happened on the beach was—"

I point at him. "I swear to God, Anthony, if you say it was a mistake, I will throttle you. Because it was as far from a mistake as humanly possible."

"It wasn't a mistake, exactly. But it—"

"*And* if you say it shouldn't have happened, that will also earn you a throttling." I step toward him. "Quit this. Quit all of it."

He stands his ground. "And what is it I'm quitting, exactly?"

Another step. "This ridiculous sense of what's right and wrong. That *you* have decided all on your own, by the way. I have no problem with it."

He opens his mouth to protest, then wisely shuts it.

I'm so close I can feel the heat of him now. "Because this?" I palm his chest, and it takes everything in me not to moan at how firm it is. "This is most definitely right."

He backs up. *Stupid man.* I follow, still touching him. Yet another step, another follow, until his back presses against the brick. His heart pounds beneath my palm, and I think it might be possible that—for a moment, at least—I'm the one in charge.

"I'll say it again," I tell him, keeping one hand on his chest and lifting the other to the top of my overalls. "I want you. I want this. Whatever it is, whatever it can be, it's what I want. I'm a grown woman, Anthony. Let me prove it to you." I unhook one side of the metal clasps, then the other, and the top falls down, revealing the white crop top I'm in.

His eyes darken, and beneath my palm, his heart speeds up. "Darcy." Suddenly, my name on his lips sounds like a warning.

I lift my brows. "Yes?"

He's deadly calm. "You have one chance to leave. One. You can walk away, and I'll pretend this never happened."

I open my mouth to protest his words, but he places a rough finger on my lips.

"This is the last time I'm going to say it. Do you understand me? Because if you stay—if you let those fucking overalls fall to the ground—you're mine. No one else's. For as long as I want you. *Mine.*"

A breath escapes me, shaky with terror and relief. Terror because he's dead serious. Relief for the same reason. There's nothing but determination in his hazel eyes, the gold flecks flashing.

He removes his finger. "Make your choice, Darcy."

I don't hesitate. "There has never been any choice except the one that leads to you." With that, I release the overalls.

On a groan, he snaps, pulling me to him in a rough embrace that feels more like he's holding onto a life raft than anything. His mouth slants over mine, and I open for him, ready for whatever he wants. He controls the kiss the same as he controlled it on the beach: a sensual determination that speaks of experience. Of desire. Of everything I have always wanted, and am quickly realizing I have never truly experienced.

"Shirt off," I murmur around his lips.

He breaks our kiss long enough to pull the fabric over his head, and I drink in the sight of him. The massive expanse of skin, the colorful, chaotic ink that decorates it, the dusting of hair that he doesn't shave. I press my lips to his chest, breathing in his scent—something woodsy, but also distinctly *Anthony*—and following it with kisses.

He allows it for all of three seconds before he's lifting me into his arms and taking me to the bedroom.

"There's a whole loft out there, and you're taking me in here?" I tease.

"Trust me, you're going to want to lie down for this." He

looks down at me as he says it, an expression of cockiness and lust heavy on his face.

In the bedroom, he doesn't bother shutting the door, but he holds me while he toes off his shoes. And when he lays me on the bed, it's gentle, almost sweet. Then he speaks, and all bets fly out the window.

"Are you on birth control?"

"IUD." Where is he going with this?

"When was the last time you had a partner? Tested?"

My lips quirk up. "It's been over a year, and I was tested a couple of months ago at my annual appointment. Why?"

He reaches down and yanks the overalls the rest of the way off, along with my socks and boots. His eyes travel hungrily over me, taking in the cotton briefs and tank top. I've never felt sexy in this kind of outfit, exactly, but under his gaze, I'm beginning to see what that might feel like.

"Because I'm going to fuck you bare, and I'm going to fill up that pretty cunt of yours with my cum. And it's going to stay there."

I blink. "What?"

"You heard me," he growls. "Take off your tank top."

I obey, still trying to wrap my head around what he just said.

Silently, he undoes his pants and lets them fall, then removes his socks. He stands before me in black boxer briefs, his cock straining against the cotton fabric, and his thighs flex as he watches me.

"You are such a fucking specimen," I whisper.

"Sit up and take off your bra," he says in response.

I do as he commands. "Are we not going to talk about what you just said?"

His brows knit. "Which part?"

"The part where you said you were going to—"

"Fuck you bare and fill you with my cum?"

Holy *shit*. My cheeks heat. Suddenly, I feel every bit of my age. I thought I was experienced, but maybe not.

His answering smirk is dark. Dangerous. As if all this was only a matter of time, and now that he'd been unleashed, my world would never be the same. "It's what's going to happen. I'm clean. You're clean. You're on birth control. You'll take my cum in your pussy and you'll like it." He places a knee on the mattress, his gaze almost feral. "Trust me, sweetheart—I'm only getting started. Just remember that you said yes."

I nod. I know implicitly that he'd back off if I said so. But no way am I slowing this train down. "Okay."

"Now, take off your bra. I want to see those tits," he commands.

I pretty much never wear a real bra, so it's a sports bra. And I have never felt less sexy than the next few seconds it takes to pull it off over my head. I rethink everything—how I should have waited to do this until after I'd had a shower. How I should have worn a real bra, for fuck's sake.

But all my doubts fall out of my head when I see the way he looks at me.

He runs his hand over his face, stroking his beard. "Damn, honey. You've been hiding those from me."

I laugh nervously, unsure of how to respond.

His eyes meet mine. "They're beautiful. Big and bold, with a little bit of softness in just the right spot. Just like the rest of you."

Never in my wildest dreams did I think I'd hear a man wax poetic about my breasts. But not only has it happened, but it's Anthony Hall who's said it. I fucking *swoon*.

He smirks. "I'll be worshipping those soon enough. Lose the panties. Let me see that pussy."

"You first." I don't know where the burst of bravery comes from, and I don't care. I'm just glad it's shown up.

His eyes twinkle. "You wanna see what I'm working with, Little Girl?"

I nod, my mouth dry.

"Eyes on my cock, then." He issues the demand, then slides the fabric off.

Oh, *fuck*. "Jesus."

"The name is Anthony. If you call anyone's name, it's mine." Then he chuckles darkly. "Or Daddy, of course."

I nod mutely. He's fucking huge. I mean, his whole body is huge, and I'd figured he'd be…*big*…but this is a whole other level of big. His hand grabs a hold of the shaft, wrapping his fingers around it and giving it a pump. I swallow. I might whimper, I don't know.

"Now, take your panties off." His voice is gruff, as though he's making an effort to speak.

And when I look up, sure enough, everything in his expression tells me he's doing everything he can to control himself. The cords of his neck strain, his shoulders are taut, and his entire body seems primed to attack.

Immediately I go hot, my already heated core going molten with desire. It's *me* he wants to attack.

I tuck my fingers into the pale pink cotton fabric and raise my hips to slide them down, watching his face the entire time. His jaw is clenched, and his eyes never leave my body. When I discard them, he speaks.

"Spread your legs, Darcy. Show me what I get to taste."

My God, this man. Pulse racing, my breath coming in pants, I let my knees fall apart.

It's terrifying. In all my times with other men, none have lingered on any part of me. Sex has been simply serviceable. With the exception of that night on the beach, I've never come except by my own ministrations, and no one has actually done what he seems primed to do.

"Look at you," he says. "So beautiful. Wet and glistening, just for me." His eyes roam lazily from my core up to my breasts before meeting my eyes. "I bet you taste as good as you smell."

I hitch a breath, not knowing how to act or what to say.

He growls, the sound one of deep satisfaction as he puts his other knee on the bed and lowers down, crawling to me on the mattress. I clench my fists as he moves slowly, his eyes surveying every inch of me as he moves.

My thoughts spiral. *I should have shaved my legs. When was the last time I trimmed my pussy? This was a bad idea. I'm out of my league.*

"Tell me something."

His words snap me back to reality. To the fact of him hovering above me, his hazel eyes searching my face as his immense body blocks out the light. A lock of brown hair flops over his forehead, giving him a rakish look. "Is there anything you like or don't like?" The tone is gentle, probing.

How in the ever-loving hell would I know the answer to that?

He frowns slightly. "Darcy?"

"I—I don't know," I finally answer. "No one's ever asked, and I..."

The smile he gives is dazzling, throwing me completely off-guard. "Then I guess I'm the lucky bastard who gets to find out." He lowers himself down to me, and I nearly pass out at the feel of him, the weight of his body on top of mine, at the hardness of his hips and cock nestled against my soft curves.

"Promise me you'll tell me if you don't like something," he presses.

I nod, wrapping my arms around his back. "I promise."

He takes my mouth with his own, his tongue controlling every stroke, heating me back up from the momentary detour my own thoughts had led me down. His hand clasps my breast and squeezes, and I moan as his lips trail a hot, open-mouthed path down my neck and to my other breast. His mouth closes over my nipple, and I arch into him, writhing at the sensations flooding my body.

His hips thrust gently between my legs, and I scrape my nails down his back, thrilling at the answering hum he gives in response. In no time, we're a tangled mess of mouths and limbs, stroking, squeezing, moaning.

He slides down my chest and belly, kissing, touching, learning my curves with an enthusiasm I have never felt. When his head is between my thighs, his eyes close and he breathes me in. "You smell so fucking good, Darcy."

I squirm, caught between discomfort and embarrassment.

He catches my movements and growls, clearly unhappy with me. "Darcy."

"Y-yes?" Why am I nervous? The man is *between my legs*, for crying out loud. He just told me I *smelled so fucking good*. Am I insane?

Pressing a warm, large hand against the inside of my thigh, he asks, "Has no one made you come like this before?"

I press my lips together. "No one…" I blow out a breath. "No one's ever, um, been down there?"

He chuffs a laugh. "You've got to be kidding me."

I go cold at his tone, unsure how I'm supposed to react, but then he continues.

"You're telling me I'm the first one to taste you? Baby." His tone gentles, his gaze reverent as he stares at my pussy. When he lifts his eyes back to mine, they're blown with lust, only a dark green circle visible around his pupil. His hands tighten and his voice deepens as he says, "This cunt, Darcy? It's all mine. All. Mine. No one else's. Do you understand?"

"Yes," I breathe.

He shakes his head. "Yes, what?"

Fuck. I grip the bedsheets as a fresh wave of goosebumps flies over me. "Yes, Daddy."

"Good girl."

"That's so fucking hot," I breathe, utterly beside myself.

He bends his head down, then peers up at me from beneath heavy brows. "Relax, Little Girl. I'm going to be here a while."

Yeah, no way. I'm going to watch as he—

Oh.

Oh, *God*.

The flat of his tongue presses against my center, and he moans. Or maybe that's me? No, we both moan. His tongue travels up, licking me from bottom to top, and my legs immediately quiver.

"Fuck, you taste good. So damn sweet." He shifts again, wrapping one arm around my leg while the other moves to rest on my stomach.

But his tongue. Dear sweet heaven above, his *tongue*. I have never…just, holy fuck. My hips jerk and he hums. He moves to my clit, and I gasp as his tongue circles it, increasing the pressure and moving it around, focusing in on the exact right spot that I crave.

I thread my hands into his silky hair and tug. "Oh my God," I whimper. "More. Do that more."

He keeps his mouth on my clit, working it and then sucking it, my hips writhing back and forth. "There you go," he urges. "Fuck my face, Darcy."

Sounds I didn't know I could make come out of me as I do just that, holding onto his hair and jerking my hips. Pleasure swirls in my core, and as his tongue and mouth work my pussy, I detonate. The pleasure courses through me, and I scream, "Anthony!"

He keeps going, working me through the orgasm until I'm a puddle on the bed. But instead of letting me recover, he rises on his knees and looks down at me, his insane cock jutting out.

Suddenly I want nothing more than to taste it. To suck him into my mouth and hear his own moans of pleasure. But when I go to move, he shakes his head. "Not yet, sweetheart. You're going to put on fresh lipstick before you suck my cock, and I'm going to love watching you. But now I want to bury myself in that delicious pussy of yours. "

I can't say anything, rendered speechless by his words as he lowers himself onto me, one hand tracing up my side as his head dips to take a nipple into his mouth.

"Oh my God, that feels so good," I moan as his mouth sucks on it, his other hand squeezing the other. I can barely figure what to do with my hands, I'm so delirious with sensation, and when he lifts his head, I pull his mouth to mine, tasting myself on his tongue. It's fucking hot.

"Now," I whisper. "I need you. Now."

He smirks. "Thought you'd never ask." Rising onto his elbow, he notches himself at my entrance and pushes the head in.

It already feels different. I've never had anyone bare inside me.

Eyes steady on mine, he adjusts my leg to allow him better access. "You feel so good, baby. Relax. Let me in. Breathe."

I blow out, not realizing that I was holding my breath. He pushes in another inch, and I inhale again. On my exhale, he pushes in farther.

"Almost there. You're doing so good," he praises.

"You're so big," I rasp.

"I know," he smiles, then gently pushes a strand of hair away from my forehead before cupping my face. His thumb strokes my cheek. "You can take it. You were made just for me."

My body goes hot again at his words, waves of goosebumps rising as I rotate my hips. The movement opens me up a little more, and his eyes go molten.

"Fuck, baby," he grits, then, on another swirl of my hips, he thrusts all the way in.

I gasp, slamming my eyes shut at the intensity of sensations flowing around me.

"Breathe," he reminds me.

I try. I'm so full.

"Open your eyes, gorgeous," he coaxes.

My eyes find his, and even though his brow is furrowed, his entire body tensed with the effort of holding himself back, the sight of him is soothing. Immediately I relax and let myself sink into the mattress.

He lowers his mouth to mine for a gentle kiss. Then he raises up, his searing gaze meeting mine as he pulls out, and slams home.

I cry out, the feeling unlike anything I've ever experienced in my life, a riot of bliss centered low in my belly and whooshing out with every motion Anthony makes above me. I moan as his hips swirl and dip, stroking me again and again, delivering round after round of pleasure so naturally and effortlessly that I wonder why I haven't been after a man like this for my entire sexual life.

Finally used to the size of him, I meet him thrust for thrust, watching the cords of his neck go taut with movement, nearly mindless with how good he feels.

"Play with yourself," he commands.

My eyes snap to his. "What?"

He doesn't stop thrusting into me. "Put your hand on your gorgeous pussy and touch yourself. Get yourself off. Because I won't last this time. You feel way too fucking good."

I reach down to circle my clit, and the sensation is nearly overwhelming.

"There you go," he says. "This tight little cunt is going to come all over my cock, isn't it? Then I'm going to fill you up."

"Fuck," I whine, my hips losing control as he pounds into me. "Fuck, Anthony, oh my—"

Without warning, the orgasm slams into me, hot and bright.

Anthony growls, pistoning into me before stilling, and I feel his release as his cock moves. It's hot and wet, and I've never felt anything like it.

He cups my chin and delivers a punishing kiss, sliding his hips in and out more gently now, as we both come down from the orgasms. The kiss grows softer as he relaxes, a smile crossing his lips as he pulls out of me, his cum beginning to seep out. Wordlessly, he takes two fingers and pushes the cum back inside, and my hips writhe at the pleasure his fingers deliver.

Satisfied, he rolls to the side and props his head in his hands to look at me. His gaze is gentle.

I don't know what to do, but my only thought is to get up. When I try, he puts a hand on my wrist. "What do you think you're doing?"

"Going to the bathroom?" It comes out as a question.

"I didn't say I was done with you."

"But—"

His eyes narrow, but his mouth is soft as he says, "Damn, Darcy, what kind of boys have you been with before now?"

I squirm.

He sighs, and it's so dramatic it makes me smile. "We have so much work to do. But for now, let me look at you."

He runs his hand over my chest, cupping a breast before moving to my belly, laying his palm flat as he goes. When he gets to my hip, he squeezes and tugs, pulling me on to my side and closer to him so he can grab my ass. "Roll over."

I obey.

"Fuck, look at that ass," he murmurs. "Absolutely perfect. It's going to look so good when I spank it."

My eyes snap to his. They're dark and dangerous.

"I told you, Darcy. We have a lot of work to do."

Chapter 16

Anthony

I COME TO with Darcy in my arms and a smile on my lips. I should feel bad about it, but after last night, I can't find it in me to care. The woman wants me? She can have me.

My dick stirs at the memories of what we did. She's so inno-cent. So *fucking* innocent. I should feel bad for all the ways I'm going to ravage her, but much like my quickly fading guilt, I can't find it in me.

Shifting, I move so I can prop my head in my hands and look at her. She's fucking flawless. Lightly tanned skin with bikini lines from her time at the beach, breasts that are far more than a handful, a stomach I can't stop wanting to lay my head on, and her hips, thighs, and ass? My fucking *dream*. She's not a small woman other than in height, and she is perfect. Completely and totally perfect.

She stirs, blinking open sleepy eyes and smiling at me with bare lips that are still swollen from all the kissing last night. She has a little beard burn, but it's not enough to keep me from leaning to give her another kiss right now.

She melts beneath me, her soft sigh making my dick harden at the very sound of it. I push her hair away from her face to get a better look at her, and her grin gets even bigger.

"Who knew you were a cuddler, Mr. Hall?" Her voice is deeper than normal.

I give her a light scoff. "Who says *I'm* the one who was cuddling all night long?"

Her hand traces patterns on my chest. "Me. Because every time I woke up, you wrapped your arms tightly around me and wouldn't let me so much as get up to go to the bathroom."

I grunt, not sure if I'm ready to admit to that. But I release her. "You have three minutes before I expect you back in here."

Her eyes light with mischief. "And if it's longer?"

Brat. "Then I'll punish you."

She grins as she scoots out of the bed. When her eyes move about the room, clearly looking for something to put on, I shake my head. "No. Naked. Time is ticking."

A slow smile crosses her face as her gaze meets mine. "Yes, Sir."

She takes five minutes.

Which is fine, because it's time she learned her first lesson.

She starts to close the door when she comes back in, and I give a quick shake of my head. "No need." Then I sit up and rest my back against the headboard. "Come over here."

Her steps are sure, but a flicker of hesitation flashes in her eyes as she crosses the room.

"Pull the covers down, and lay beside me, on your stomach."

She steps to the bed and does as she's told, lifting the covers and pulling them all the way to the end of the bed. Her eyes widen as she takes in my swollen cock. "I don't know how it's possible, but I think I forgot just how big you were. I thought it was a fever dream."

I chuckle. "I'm no dream, sweetheart. Now lay down."

She makes her way onto the bed, and I watch with rapt fascination as she moves, her breasts hanging heavy as she lowers herself to the mattress, then folds her arms to rest her head on them as she turns her gaze towards me. Her ice-blue eyes blink innocently as she says, "Now what, Daddy?"

Oh, fuck me. I shouldn't, but God *damn* I fucking love it when she says it. And it must show on my face because she damn near purrs in satisfaction. I move, going onto my knees and running a hand along her back, down to her creamy white ass, and then down her legs. "Now you get punished for disobeying me," I answer, and without giving her even a moment to wonder what I mean, I lift my hand and bring it down on her right cheek, delivering the first spanking.

She jerks, a look of surprise on her face as her mouth opens and she makes a noise of protest.

My cock jerks with pleasure. I do it again, this time smacking the left side. And she wiggles, pressing her thighs together like she's trying to relive some pressure.

Perfect. I knew my little brat would like this. I deliver two more spanks, one for each side, watching the way her pale flesh reddens with my handprints. Groaning with the effort of not bending her over to fuck her immediately, I lean down and put my mouth next to her ear. "Feels good, doesn't it?"

She shivers, then nods. "Yes," she whispers tentatively.

"Nothing to be ashamed about," I murmur, rising back up and soothing the spots I've marked. I deliver another round, her answering moans music to my ears, then push my hand between her legs. "Fuck, you're soaked."

She whines. "Anthony, please."

With a growl, I demand, "Please *what*?"

"Please…anything," she answers, wiggling her ass.

I smack it. "Stop moving."

She stills. "Please, Daddy."

I push my hand back between her legs, reveling in her wetness. Sliding a finger between her swollen folds, I tease her entrance, giving her just a little. Her legs tense in response, and I stop. She relaxes.

"You're learning," I praise. "Good girl."

"Fuck," she breathes. "Why is that so hot?"

I reward her with my finger, and she moans again.

"Can I have another?" she asks.

"Another what?"

"Spanking." She's not quiet about it this time.

My dick leaks at the request. I thought for sure she meant another finger, but this sweet innocent girl wants another spanking?

I pull my finger out of her pussy and present it to her. "Suck."

She opens her mouth without complaint, and when her soft mouth wraps around my finger, I nearly come right then and there. I don't miss the smirk on her lips as she licks me clean, either. She releases my finger with a pop as I slide it out of her mouth, and I move swiftly to give her exactly what she—and I— are desperate for.

Smack.

"Fuck, Daddy," she breathes, her hands balled into fists on the mattress. "Again."

"Seems someone likes herself a little pain to go with the pleasure I'm about to give." I bring my hand down on the other side, watching with satisfaction as the skin continues to redden, then soothing it with slow circles.

"Again."

"No," I respond. "You aren't the one in charge here, Darcy." I grab her by the hip and yank, rolling her onto her back, her tits wiggling.

She looks up at me, her eyes bright. "What are you going to do to me?"

I don't answer. Instead, I pull her leg up and around to bracket my hips, then yank her to me. Her chest heaves. "Yes, please."

Still without speaking, I grab a pillow and put it beneath her hips, then lean over her. "Ready to be fucked, Little Girl?"

Her answering laugh is low and dark. "Do your worst."

I slam home, both of us moaning. She's so fucking tight around me, probably swollen from last night's activities, and it's that much better. I pull back and thrust again, needing to fuck her like I need to breathe. Her tits move with the force of my thrusts, and I lean down to capture one in my mouth, sucking the nipple in and biting down.

"Ow, *fuck!*" she yelps.

I don't stop. She'll take it.

Sure enough, her arms wrap around me, pulling me closer even as I pound harder, sucking her nipple much more intently. No way am I going to last.

"Yes, yes, yes," she chants. "Harder, Anthony. Harder."

I'm feral, growling and rutting into her with a ferocity I'm not sure I've ever felt. My balls tighten, my back tingles, and I know I'm nearing the edge.

"Come for me, Darcy. I need you to come. Now."

The command works. She flutters around my cock, her sweet sounds driving me faster and harder.

She yells with her orgasm, her nails scraping down my back in a painfully delicious move that has me hissing in pleasure. I come instantly, growling into the curve of her neck as I hold her leg tight against my hip. She arches into me, a string of words and noises I don't quite understand, but that I love.

Slowly, we still, and she holds me tight to her.

"That was amazing," she finally says, her words slurred as though she's drunk.

I chuckle. "It better have been." Then I pull out, my cum leaking out of her as I go. It's sexy as fuck, and I lazily push it back inside, swirling it into her like I did last night.

When I let myself flop onto the mattress onto my back, and

Darcy follows, nestling her head onto my chest and humming contentedly.

It's nice. I probably shouldn't like it as much as I do, because God knows this can't be anything other than what this is, but I'm a selfish bastard, so I'll enjoy it for however long she lets me.

Then her stomach growls, and she giggles. "Sorry."

I press a quick kiss to her forehead and tap her side, then get up. She rolls over and rises, as well. "Come on. Shower and then I'll feed you."

She waggles her eyebrows. "You gonna feed me, or are you gonna *feed me*?"

I level her with my best glare. "You need to eat, Darcy."

She just giggles in response. "Okay, Daddy."

I roll my eyes and lead the way to the shower.

"Damn, that's a fine sight," Darcy says behind me. "Is this what I miss every morning? You striding naked across your loft?"

I give her a wink over my shoulder as I walk. "You should know, stalker."

She blushes, and it's the best thing I've ever seen. "Shut up."

"Tell me I'm wrong."

"You're wrong," she protests behind me.

A snort escapes me. "Nice try."

She hums again, this one a noise of protest. How is it I already know the difference in her hums?

In the bathroom, ironically the only space other than the kitchen that she *hasn't* redone in some way yet, I turn the shower on and swivel to face her. "I don't have much in here. Soap and… soap."

She shrugs. "It's okay, Anthony. Not like you planned on needing girl soap." She smiles.

We step into the stream, and I grab the bar of soap before she can, using it as another opportunity to run my hands over her luscious curves. She rinses and takes the soap from me, lathering me up the same as I did to her: with relish, and not missing a single inch.

"My stomach growled again," she giggles as we dry off.

"Seems you've worked up an appetite." I grin at her.

Her own smile broadens in response.

"Put on one of my shirts," I tell her, opening the bathroom door and moving across the wide-open space once again.

"That's not necessary," she protests behind me.

I turn back to her. "It wasn't an offer, Darcy. It was a command."

She laughs. "You're funny."

I grunt, ignoring the comment and deciding she'll understand I'm serious soon enough. Grabbing her clothes before she has time to get into the room, I sweep them into a drawer and hold out a T-shirt as she walks in.

"Where are my clothes?"

"I told you that you're wearing one of my shirts."

"But—my panties…"

"Are unnecessary."

"And bra?"

"*Definitely* not needed." I pause. "Is that even comfortable?"

"What, the sports bra?" she clarifies.

I nod.

She snorts. "Of course not. But that's the breaks," she says and shrugs.

An irrational anger rises in me. The desire to take manufac-turers to task and force them to make it better. She shouldn't ever be uncomfortable.

"Anway, this seems unfair," she continues. "Me only in a shirt and you in, what, a full set of clothes? Where's *my* joy, Mr. Hall?"

I pull on a pair of boxers and hold my arms out. "Fair?"

She crosses her arms, looking absolutely delectable as she stands before me, still naked, tits on full display as she scowls at me. "I'd rather you be in briefs. Got any tighty whities in there?"

I smirk. She probably thinks I don't own them. But I'm going to go one better. "Fine." I shuck the boxers off and extract a pair of leopard-print briefs, then pull them on to her absolute delight. Letting the elastic snap against my waist, I strike a pose for her. "Is this joyful enough, Darcy?"

She covers her mouth and laughs. "It is, without a doubt, the most spectacular sight I have ever seen in my entire life."

"Enjoy it, then. But no bacon for you."

Her pretty lips open in surprise. "There's bacon?"

"There *was* bacon," I correct. "No way am I going to cook it like this."

If I thought she was cute before, then the pout she gives me now might be the thing that undoes me. "Come on," she wheedles.

I pop a smack on her bare ass as I walk past. "No."

She brews the coffee while I make us scrambled egg and avocado breakfast tacos, and she shivers as she sits on the wooden chair at the small table set just off the kitchen.

"Cold?"

She pins me with a glare. "When was the last time you sat your bare ass on a chair?"

Okay, that's fair. But I need her without panties. With a sigh, I pull my briefs off and sit, wincing as my balls attempt a retreat into my body. "Happy?"

She blinks. "First, you produce a pair of *leopard-print briefs*, and then you doff them to sit bare-assed on a chair like me. Who the fuck are you, and what did you do with Anthony Hall?"

I use my fork to indicate the food in front of her. "Eat. When we're done, I have more eating to do."

Her eyes widen, but she does as she's told. She tries to wash the dishes when we finish, but I reach around and turn the water off. "No."

"You cooked," she protests, turning to look at me.

I close the few inches and kiss her, tasting the too-sweet

coffee she drinks. Without a word, I scoop her into my arms and walk us back to the table, sitting her on top and kneeling before her. Hurts my knees like a motherfucker, but considering I'm about to bury my tongue in her pussy, I'll get over it.

"Anthony, what are you—ohhh," she moans, losing all coherent sounds as I lick and stroke her. She's trimmed, the black hair framing the prettiest pussy I've ever seen. Georgia O'Keefe herself would have been inspired.

"Look at you," I say, the taste of her fresh on my tongue. "Spread out like a damn feast just for me."

I dive back between her legs, her mewls and sighs growing louder and louder until I've made her come. I barely let her recover before I'm standing and thrusting my cock into her, unable to believe how fucking good she still feels. It can't possibly stay like this, my insatiable need to be inside her constantly. But as I stroke us to another set of orgasms, listening to her deep groans of pleasure, as I lift her legs to rest on my shoulders so I can get a better angle and watch her body move, just as sexy covered by my plain white T-shirt as if she were bare, I have to wonder what the fuck I'm doing.

But now isn't the time for introspection. Now is the time to make her come. I press my thumb onto her clit, and sure enough, she cries out as her inner walls contract around me.

"Holy shit, oh my God, Anthony!" she screams as she comes. I hold off, waiting until I know she's through before letting myself go. "Lift your shirt," I grit out, and she does. Right in time for me to pull out and spurt all over her, long ropes of cum as she lifts onto her elbows to watch.

"Fuck yes, Anthony. Come all over me," she urges. "Fucking paint my stomach."

I swear, her words have me coming even more. All I can do is come, and come, and come.

Finally, I'm spent, and a wave of dizziness overtakes me.

Using a hand to brace myself on the table, I take a deep breath and finally meet her eyes. "Holy shit."

She eases her legs off my shoulders and smirks. "Holy shit is right, Mr. Hall. That was fucking incredible."

I steal a glance at the clock across the room, then groan at the time. "I need to get downstairs."

She sits up, her legs dangling off the table.

"I'm going to rinse off, but if you want another shower..." I start.

She shakes her head. "I want to feel this all day. Well, except for the cum. *That* I'll rinse off."

We take care of things, and I pull her clothes out of the drawer I'd stashed them in.

"Where's my underwear?"

"I'm keeping those."

Her eyes shimmer. "You gonna wash them or...?"

"See you downstairs."

"Hey—um," she starts.

Instantly I sense a shift in the mood, and I stiffen.

"What...what is this?" Darcy waves her hands between the two of us.

Tension takes up residence between my shoulders. "Why does it have to be anything?"

She stares at me. "I just—"

I take another step back, fighting the instinct that wants nothing more than to take her in my arms and offer comfort. "I just had my tongue buried in your pussy not half an hour ago. There's no need to define this."

"So, we're just...hooking up?" Her voice sounds small.

Hell. Isn't this what *she* wants? No way would she want more than that. I'm old as fuck compared to her. So I shove the voice that's yelling I'm being an asshole far, far down, and I nod. I nearly buckle when I raise my eyes to hers and see the pain she's trying so fucking hard to cover up. But that doesn't make any sense. Why would she want *me*? I'm good for a roll in the hay. Not much else.

"Okay," she responds.

I turn and walk as nonchalantly as possible, willing myself to move forward.

CHAPTER 17

DARCY

TWO DAYS. JUST two days ago, the growly man behind the bar was fucking me like our lives depended on it, and I can't stop thinking about it. About him. About how different he is when it's just us, the way he grants me grin after grin, as though he isn't giving me a precious gift every single time.

Good lord. Am I comparing his smiles to "precious gifts" now? I really am dick-whipped.

To be honest, no one would blame me. Amanda sure doesn't, because I called her almost the second that he left me in his loft two mornings ago.

Suffice to say that my girl is a big believer in whatever is happening.

Anthony and I haven't had any time together since that morning two days ago. I've been putting in extra time at Dad's hardware store in the morning and night helping to train the summer part-time students, putting me in Anthony's loft long after he's left for the morning and leaving before he's done for the night. Never mind the work I'm doing on the pool table in Agatha's garage. Part of me is glad for the time apart, because I can't help the twinge of unease every time I think about the way we ended things the other day. The other part of me wants to climb him like a tree and demand he do that thing with his tongue again.

I know I should be fine with the set-up we agreed to—who gets mad about hook-ups that are like Anthony Hall?—but I want more. Which is a "me" problem, I know.

Throwing my car into park, I grab my things before sauntering across the sweltering parking lot and into the cool dimness of Hall's Balls. I take a moment to let my eyes adjust to the light, using the time to reset. There's no escaping Anthony tonight, because it's bowling league night. I left my work in the loft early and went home to shower and shave. And…maybe I put on a nice bra and panties, and maybe I didn't. Who's to say?

My hair is up in its customary top knot, a pink bandana tied around it. I'm in my pink cheetah crop top and wearing a just-below-the-knee black skirt that is stretchy and comfortable as hell. I distinctly recall the way Anthony's eyes tracked me in this skirt the last time I wore it, and I plan on using every tool in my arsenal to get back into his bed tonight. Because I do, in fact, want to climb him like a tree and demand he do that thing with his tongue again.

His eyes flit to me once he's finished with a group of moms who had far more to say to him than necessary. I know it's terrible of me, but I absolutely love that he gave them exactly no attention other than the bare minimum to get their drinks and process payment. I don't know that I'm jealous of them, exactly, but I'm not going to lie and say that there's something about how free they seem to feel about flirting with him that I don't think I could get away with.

He nears me, and I smile. "Hey, Mr. Hall."

"Drink?" The way he's acting, it's as though the man hasn't had his mouth on me.

"Pitcher of margaritas, please," I say, leaning onto the bar and making sure to give him the full benefit of my low-cut top.

And…score! It works. He glances down for the briefest of seconds and I cheer inside my head. When his gaze meets mine again, his eyes are heated.

"What is that?" he growls.

I tilt my head. "What is what?"

He moves infinitesimally closer. "What are you wearing?"

Ah. "A bra."

He grunts, which makes me laugh.

"A margarita, please." I pause. "Top shelf."

His eyes meet mine. With another grunt, he turns to put it together.

"Hi!" comes a voice from beside me. I turn, and there's Devon and Aaron. Devon wraps me in a tight hug, then nods a hello at the stone-faced Anthony.

He slides the margarita to me, then raises a questioning brow at Devon and Aaron.

"Me, too!" Amanda says, sliding up next to me with Agatha in tow.

I wince. "Was I supposed to bring you?"

Agatha waves my concern away. "Not at all. Amanda and I had some planning to do."

Devon takes a sip of the drink Anthony slid to her. "Planning? Or plotting? Because I know your type, Agatha—and there's always something going on in that head of yours that the rest of us have no clue about.

Beside her, Aaron laughs. "Isn't that the truth."

"You play the long game—and I should know," Devon continues, looking at her husband with a knowing smile.

Agatha clasps her hands in front of her chest. "That sounds like a story I'd love to know."

I lean in. "Same. Spill it, sister."

Devon laughs. "Let's just say that my grandmother made it

her mission to get me and Aaron together, even though at the time I was traveling the country and had no plans to come home to Talladega."

"But come home she did, and it gave me the chance I needed to prove she should be with me," Aaron says, pulling Devon's back to him and kissing her cheek.

"That's adorable," Amanda coos.

"Sounds like your grandmother is pretty amazing," I add.

"She was," Devon says.

After a beat, I clap my hands. "Okay, let's get our bowling on, shall we?"

The four of us head to the lane closest to the bar and get situated, swapping out our shoes and picking our balls. I'm the only one who's bothered to buy her own bowling ball, and of course it's a cherry red, marbled through with streaks of pearl. We enter our names into the scoreboard, and as I glimpse Anthony behind us, I wonder for the first time if he's always put us in this lane on purpose.

Nah. No way.

But…maybe?

Whatever. I'm being silly.

Halfway through our first game, I've just bowled a bucket, taking down the 2, 4, 5, and 8 pins, when Anthony walks out from the bar and comes over to us.

"Are you taking drink orders over here now?" Amanda teases.

She knows good and damn well that Anthony Hall would do no such thing. Which begs the question.

"You're doing it wrong." He nearly snarls the words, and then I realize he's holding a bowling ball bag.

No way.

I point to it. "Do you…bowl?"

He gives me a *what do you think* look, his lips flat behind his thick beard. "Yes."

My jaw unhinges, but at the same time, of course he bowls. *Of course* he does. The man is a freaking onion, revealing layer after painstaking layer as slow as molasses in winter. And for as frustrating as it is—as *he* is—all it really makes me want to do is uncover more.

More. When it comes to Anthony Hall, I simply want *more*.

Agatha claps. "Are you going to give us a lesson?"

Devon's eyes light up with mischief as she looks between Anthony and me. "Start now. Darcy's got one more bowl. Maybe she needs some hands-on help."

Amanda snorts behind me, but Anthony doesn't so much as look at Devon. His eyes are glued to mine, and I have no idea what is happening right now.

"Get up here."

I don't hesitate. Distantly, I wonder if I should be so quick to do what he says, but honestly, I don't care. If Anthony Hall wants to give me bowling lessons, then I am all for Anthony Hall giving me bowling lessons. Any damn day of the week.

Behind me, it sounds like Agatha and Devon are grilling Amanda to get the skinny on why the town grump is suddenly out from behind the bar and willingly engaging in conversation with a customer. But I don't care. Because in front of me Anthony is pulling out a sixteen-pound ball with the largest finger holes I have ever seen in a ball…and the jokes really write themselves here, but I keep my snickering to myself.

"Your approach is wrong."

"O-kay," I answer, drawing the word out.

"You need to stand just off-center. Not there. There. And your follow-through is shit. You're right-handed, so you need to step off with your left foot. You need to be pulling your arm back as you walk, and then letting the ball go as your right foot hits the line. You're not aiming straight for the center—you pretty much never want to do that." He pauses. "Are you listening to me?"

I drag my eyes from his chest and meet his glare, barely suppressing a grin. "Sorry. Were you talking?"

He huffs. "Darcy."

I chuckle. "I'm listening, Mr. Hall. Keep going."

And I see it. The faintest tip up of his lips, even though to anyone else it looks like he's scowling.

"Wanna show me how it's done?" I continue.

"Finish your frame," he answers. "Then I'll do the next one."

Keeping his brief instructions in my mind, I back up and take my turn. The ball releases and lands about a quarter of the way down the lane, off to the center and rolling toward the four pins that remain from my first bowl. When the ball hits them, it takes down all but one.

"Yes!" I pump my fist in victory. It's a great turn, as far as I'm concerned.

Anthony is less than impressed, but of course, that doesn't surprise me in the least. The few times I've seen anything approaching something other than scowling is when he's naked above me.

Focus, Darcy.

The pins reset and Anthony turns to the other three women. "The first thing to know about bowling is that it's all about your approach and follow-through. How much action you can get on the ball, and how far you can get it down the lane. The other thing to know is how slick the lanes themselves are, but unless you're walking up to feel the lane itself, there's not much you can know."

"And how slick are your lanes, Anthony?" I ask, knowing that it sounds incredibly sexual and not caring in the slightest.

He levels a look at me. "Very. Especially this one. I make sure that this lane is freshly oiled for the four of you every week."

"Seriously?" Devon asks. "But we're not even that good."

"I know, and I'm beginning to take personal offense," Anthony retorts.

Amanda laughs. "Holy shit, did you just make a joke?"

He scowls at her. "No."

She laughs harder. "Yes, you did."

I bite back a smile. He is dead serious about this lesson, that much is clear. And taking such care of us with the lane? *Dammit, Anthony.* He can't be like this and expect me to keep my cool. I clear my throat. "Keep going, Anthony. What else?"

He launches in, talking more about stance, form, rotation, spin, and so on. Finally, he steps back and takes his turn, releasing the ball with a punishing throw that lands it, no kidding, halfway down the damn lane. The sound of the ball hitting the pins is a loud *crack* that causes everyone at the other lanes to look over. Meanwhile, the four of us cheer and whoop, because of course, he bowls a strike. And when the pins reset and he takes his second turn, he does it again and bowls a spare. "It's that easy," he says, retrieving his ball from the chute and plucking a towel out of his back pocket to wipe it clean.

"Well," Agatha says, "Seems we'll need a few more lessons from you if we're going to be ready for this competition in three months."

He raises a brow. "You're going to a competition?"

I nod. "In Mobile."

He sighs. "We have a lot of work to do."

"It's just for fun, Anthony," Devon pipes up. "But the lessons are great. It's my turn—tell me how I can do this better." She steps up and Anthony watches her.

Half an hour later, we've all received personalized guidance from Anthony, and he's gone back behind the bar.

Devon turns to me. "Ahem. What's going on there?"

"What's going on where?" I ask, hopefully sounding as inno-cent as possible.

"Between you and the bartender," Agatha says. "Which is too bad, because I had a really nice young man I wanted to introduce you to."

Repressing the shiver at the idea of Agatha setting me up with someone, I continue. "There's nothing going on."

Amanda widens her eyes at me, but Agatha and Devon can't see her.

"Well, if there isn't anything going on with you two, then maybe there should be," Devon teases, her eyes on the bar behind me. "He's nice."

He's nice all right. Especially his mouth. And his hands. And holy shit, his cock. But I don't say any of that.

Agatha titters. "I don't know if I'd call him nice, dear, but he sure looks like he could throw you around in bed."

I nearly choke on the dregs of my margarita. "Excuse me?"

She rolls her eyes and doesn't bother responding.

Devon and Amanda cackle. Devon says, "I have a brother-in-law like him. Still waters run deep, that's all I'm saying."

I swear, between her and her husband, I'm beginning to think those two have a whole story or five to tell.

"Come on." I step up to reset the scoreboard. "One more round?"

Chapter 18

Darcy

AFTER BOWLING, I head home. It's still early, and as delightful as it might be to watch Anthony tend bar and ogle his ass, I have things to do. I head out to the garage, the latest order from my so-tiny-it-barely-exists business burning a hole in my brain. It's nothing huge, but I keep reminding myself that even the biggest companies started out small.

Tonight's order is for Devon and Aaron, and pretty straightforward. They want a Shaker-inspired table, but I'll put a few subtle design elements in there that will make it uniquely mine: where a Shaker design is all straight lines, I'll throw a rounded edge in there, maybe a leaf-inspired design going down the top third of the legs. Nothing that's too intense, but enough so that when you stop to look at it, all you can think is how beautiful it is.

I throw on some Noah Kahan and set to it, donning my goggles and turning the lathe on to begin shaping one of the legs. It isn't until I've sanded the piece and turned the lathe off that I realize someone is in here with me, and I turn to see none other than Anthony, watching me with that signature grumpy look of his.

What's interesting is that at this point, I know that this is simply the way he looks when he's studying something intently. He's not mad or even grumpy, exactly; he's simply observing.

"Hey, Mr. Hall," I grin over at him and nestle my goggles on the top of my head.

He stays where he is, propped against the garage opening with his arms crossed over his massive chest. His hazel eyes study me. "Hi."

My lips lift. "What brings you to my side of the world?"

"A guy can't come over to see you without getting the third degree?"

I snort. "One question does not the third degree make."

He shrugs and lets that one movement tell me everything he thinks about my statement. After a moment, he continues, "What are you making?"

"A table." I glance back at the lathe before meeting his assessing gaze again. "Working on one of the legs, but I don't think I got it right. I'll try again tomorrow." I was going to try again tonight, but Anthony being here is *far* more interesting.

He steps into the garage, clearly wanting my permission to get closer. I motion him over, hoping he doesn't ask what's under the enormous sheet. Because that's his, and I'm nowhere near ready for him to see it yet. Hell, I'm not ready for him to even know what it is.

"Looks perfect to me," he says now, looking down at the length of oak held in the lathe's bracings.

"Of course it looks perfect to you," I joke. "You don't know what you're looking at." As the words leave my mouth, I think that maybe I shouldn't have been so cavalier.

He isn't fazed. "You're right," he admits. "It's impressive. Whether you got it right is something only you'd know."

"Oh, anyone would know once all four legs were on the table," I point out. "Trust me."

He looks at me, and it's only then that I realize how close he's gotten. We're not even a foot apart, his eyes a dark green and blue in the dimmer light of the garage. I clench my hand into a fist, commanding myself not to reach for him, to stroke his beard and feel its rough bristles beneath my palm.

Because I want to. So badly. And I shouldn't want him as much as I do. I'm smart enough to know that this isn't supposed to be…something. The problem, of course, is that I can't get that message to my heart from my brain.

"You know," I start, "Agatha's going to see your car out there and know you're here. She'll figure us out if she hasn't already."

He shrugs again. "I don't care."

I frown. "You don't care what she thinks? You know what a gossip she is, right?"

He huffs the tiniest of laughs. "Darcy, if you knew all the town gossip I knew. I just keep it all here." He taps his head. "But no. I don't care what she thinks. I don't care what anyone thinks."

He steps closer. I worry my lip. "But…*no one*? Not even…" *Am I really about to say this?* "Not even your parents?"

His expression softens as he reaches to brush a strand of hair behind my ear. "No. I stopped worrying about that a long time ago." Then he grins, and my heart stutters. "Are you telling me that *you*, Darcy Belle, are worried about what others think?"

Heat flames my cheeks. "I don't know," I answer him honestly. "Maybe if I had a better understanding of what we're actually doing here, I'd be a bit more…settled."

"Why do you need an answer to that so quickly?" he counters.

Now *I'm* the one shrugging.

"Tell you what," he offers. "Why don't you let me take you inside your house and make you come." He smiles wickedly. "That should put you at ease for the night, at least."

I stare up at him. "You're dead serious, aren't you?"

"About making you come? Abso-fucking-lutely." Then, without warning, he picks me up and tosses me over his shoulders.

"Anthony!" I yelp. "Oh my God, put me down!"

"Next time your feet touch the floor is when I say so, Darcy Belle, and not a moment before."

I smack at his back, but I may as well be a fly bothering a horse for all the good it does me. He spanks my ass with a pop, and God, it feels so good. Why does getting spanked feel so delicious? I wiggle more. "Put me down!"

Another spanking, which is exactly what I'm aiming for.

He chuckles as he opens the door to my cottage. "Seems like someone wants to be punished."

I writhe in his grip, half excited and half terrified, as he stalks through the tiny house.

In the bedroom, Anthony walks to the bed and lowers us down so he's sitting and my face is inches from the mattress. "I'm letting you go, but only so you can get naked. And Darcy?"

I don't answer.

He spanks me.

"Yes?"

"First, you answer me when I ask a question. Second, you will stand in front of me and strip yourself bare, and you will do nothing but that until I give you permission to do otherwise. Am I clear?"

I grin, my heartbeat racing. "Crystal."

He levers me off his shoulder, guiding my feet to the floor and steadying me with his hands on my hips, while the blood rushes out of my head and I get my bearings. The heat in his hazel eyes is unmistakable. *He really wants me.* And it's heady, the power I feel. Slowly, I unsnap my dusty overalls, letting them fall open before stepping out of my work boots and pulling my socks off. I slide the overalls off, kicking them to the side, my gaze never leaving his face all the while.

He's leaning back on his hands, his eyes hooded with need, his jaw ticking occasionally as I reveal more and more skin. But it's the outfit I'm in now, the yellow lace bra and panty set I wore to give him a show at the bowling alley, that makes him growl. Low, predatory. My skin prickles at the sound.

"Told you I was wearing a bra," I say, sounding deliberately bratty to get the best rise out of him.

He meets my eyes. "Take it off. Leave the panties."

I reach behind my back and unhook the bra, a sigh of relief immediately coming out as it comes undone, releasing my breasts.

"Doesn't that feel better?" he asks.

"You have no idea." Damn things are torture. I much prefer my usual sports bras.

"Turn around."

I obey, dropping the bra to the floor as I go.

And this man's hands come up to my back, and he lightly scratches where the instrument of torture has been. The moan that comes out of my mouth…at this moment, it's better than any orgasm he's delivered.

He chuckles. "Thought so."

Do I say it? "But don't you like it?" I can't keep the hint of vulnerability out of my voice.

"Of course I like it. Your tits are amazing, Darcy, and that bra made sure I could tell."

"But?"

"But it was clearly uncomfortable. Besides, I don't care what you wear. I know what's underneath." He pulls me backward so his arms can wrap around and cup my breasts. When he speaks, his breath fans the skin of my back. "I know where the freckles are. What color nipples you have. The way they tighten just for me when I do this." He runs his hands over them, pinching them while nipping at my back. I moan again, more of a plea than anything. Then he releases me. "Take one step forward."

I obey.

"Bend over. I want to see just how pretty your ass is."

I hesitate, hoping for a punishment.

"Brat," he says, amusement lacing his tone. "Do as I say."

I look over my shoulder. His eyes are glued to my ass, and they flick up to meet mine for a brief second. "*Now*, Darcy, or the punishment won't be what you want, I assure you."

I raise a brow. "Maybe it will be."

But I do as he commands, bending to present myself to him, and even though I'm still wearing panties, it feels like I've never been more exposed.

"Fucking gorgeous," he murmurs, his hands moving around my ass. When he's had his fill, he tells me to stand, and he slides my panties off, his beard scraping against my skin as he goes.

"Lay over my knees."

I startle. "What?"

He tilts his head. "You heard me, Miss Belle." He pats his knee. "Put your pretty body across my knees. You're about to be spanked."

Fuck. Immediately, my pussy gets wet, and I can feel the dampness between my legs. Need courses through me and I do exactly as instructed, despite it feeling a little odd.

"Comfortable?" he asks.

"Um-hmm," I answer.

"Good." A second later, he spanks me.

"Fuck," I exhale, luxuriating in the way his hand circles the spot he's hit.

He spanks me again, and again, and again, his grunts blending with mine, until I'm a writhing, needy mess.

"Please, Daddy," I beg. "I need you."

"What do you need?" His hand moves between my legs, but nowhere near the area I'm desperate for.

"I need you to fuck me." I wiggle, desperate for more.

"You're so sexy like this. Do you know that?" His voice is husky, and I can feel his cock pressing against my side. "So fucking needy, your ass red from my hands. Get on the bed on all fours."

I hurry to comply, turning my head to watch him undress. I'll never get over he way he looks, solid muscle on solid muscle. This man has absolutely ruined me for anyone younger.

Hell, he's ruined me for any other man, period. I have no idea how I'm supposed to be done with him.

"You like what you see?" he asks.

"Fuck yes," I breathe. He still hasn't let me do anything to him. "Can I suck you?"

"Shit, baby, when you ask me so prettily like that, your ass in my face…turn around. You can have my cock."

My pussy throbs again as I reposition myself on the mattress, and I press my legs together to get some relief. He's tall enough that I stay on my knees, bent over, to lift his cock to my lips. With my eyes firmly glued to his, I lick the precum off the tip, then move my tongue over my lips. I moan. "Thank you."

His eyes flare.

Then I open my mouth and take him in, slowly, working him as though my mouth can't take it. But it very much can. I just want to draw this out as long as possible.

"More, Darcy," he commands.

I take him deeper, listening to his answering groan, then pull away and do it again, hollowing my cheeks as I pull up. Fuck. I need relief. I pop off him.

"You need my cock in that pretty cunt of yours, don't you?"

I whimper and nod, not caring about anything except getting him inside me.

"Turn around. Give me your ass, baby."

I obey, but when I move to put myself closer to him, he smacks my ass. I lower my head and moan. "Please."

He snakes a hand between my legs, finding my clit and barely touching it. I hiss, then wiggle, desperate for any friction. His hand withdraws and I whimper again.

"*Please*, Daddy. Please. I need your cock inside me. I need you to fill me up."

One hand grips my hip as he lines himself up behind me. I barely manage to stay still but can't keep the needy moan inside.

"You want this cock?"

I nod vigorously. "Yes, please, my God, *please*."

He thrusts in, hard, and I nearly come right then. The size of him stings for a second, but it only makes the following pleasure that much better.

"Fuck, Darcy. Your cunt is so fucking perfect." He does it again, harder, both of us moaning. The sounds he makes, low and just as needy as me, send me racing to the edge. More and more he fucks me, both hands on my hips as he gives me what I need—what we *both* need.

The only sound in the room is the sound of our sex. Panting. Skin on skin. The thrust of his cock into my dripping wet pussy. I moan, surrendering to him completely, balling the fitted sheet in my hands so hard it pulls off the mattress.

Behind me, Anthony groans. "Your cunt is so good, baby. Made to take this cock." He shifts and slides his hand up my back, pushing me wordlessly down to the bare mattress. My cheek presses against the rough fabric as he grunts behind me, the angle so deep it's almost painful.

It's incredible. Rough, feral, *incredible*.

"There you go," he praises. "I can feel you tighten around my cock," Anthony rasps behind me, not slowing down. "Come for me."

But I don't want to. I want more. I don't want this to stop. My body barrels forward without care as I draw up onto my elbows, the orgasm blooming from deep inside me. I shake with the release, crying out.

Anthony groans with his own release, losing his rhythm before slamming into me and stilling, his cock twitching as his fingers press divots into my hips. "So good," he pants, then bends and places the sweetest of kisses on me, peppering them from one shoulder to the other.

I hum in response, unable to do more than revel in the post-orgasmic bliss.

"So fucking perfect," he rasps, then pulls out. "The prettiest picture, you bent over with my cum trickling down your leg." He delivers a light smack on my ass, then says, "Stay there. I'll be right back."

My legs shake with the effort of staying upright, but in moments, he's back with a wet washcloth, cleaning me gently. The care and attention of it surprises me, even though I should have expected it.

When he's finished, he puts the washcloth in the hamper and we set the fitted sheet back to rights, then we climb into the bed and he tucks me to him, little spoon to big spoon. He kisses my shoulder and whispers, "Go to sleep," and my eyes prick with unwelcome emotion. I've never been cuddled like this. Never felt the heaviness of an arm settle on top of me as someone drifts into sleep. Never had someone who could both command me and care for me.

I stay awake long into the night, reveling in the way our bodies fit against each other, the sound of his breathing, and the feel of simply being wanted. Eventually, I drift off to sleep, and when I wake up in the morning, I find he's gone.

CHAPTER 19

ANTHONY

WHEN DARCY SHOWS up on Saturday, I'm already waiting for her. Her surprise is evident, and I can't decide if I'm insulted by it, or simply happy that I'm the first one who's ever given her the attention and care she deserves. She's mentioned only one guy before, Jason, and it sounds like he was a douche.

She skids to a halt in the doorway, a thermos in one hand and her tote filled to the brim with who knows what. With a pointed glance at the table that's seemed to get worse for wear this past month, she asks, "What's all this?"

"This is breakfast before you start working," I answer simply. Then I pull the chair out and gesture for her to have a seat.

The smile she gives me, pure and delighted, stabs into my heart with something I don't want to investigate. "You made me breakfast?"

"I'm helping you today, too. For a few hours, at least." I push her chair in, then head to the kitchen.

"How do you know I haven't eaten already?" she calls out.

I snort. The woman never eats in the morning, even though

it's clear she needs it. She's always happier, her focus and efforts better, when she does.

When I set the plate in front of her, she gasps. "You…made waffles?" Then she giggles. "And you put a strawberry and blueberry smiley face on mine?"

"What's the point of waffles if you can't make a face with them?"

Her answering laugh is brighter than the sunshine streaming through the windows. "I'm almost sad to ruin this masterpiece, Anthony, but I love fruit. And waffles."

I cut my own up and watch as she takes her first bite. The moan she gives is enough to make me want to throw her over my shoulder and have my way with her. Forget the work that has to be done today. She's closed her eyes, the fork held in the air as though she can't be bothered to move it while she's so focused on the bite, and there's a bit of syrup on the side of her mouth that is positively sinful.

Finally, she swallows and opens her eyes, pinning me with those bright aqua blues as she licks the syrup off. "I can't believe any of this."

I chew my forkful before asking, "Believe what?"

She gestures with her hand. "All of this. You cooked me breakfast. You made waffles. With a cute little smiley face on it. And bacon. You made *bacon*." She shoves half a piece in her mouth and it's the hottest thing I've ever seen. "You, Anthony Hall, are sweet."

I bristle. "I am no such thing."

She cackles at my reaction. "Oh, you most definitely are. And no one knows it but me." Her eyes soften as she reaches for the coffee I've made exactly how she likes it. "Thank you."

My face warms, and I clear my throat. "You're welcome. It's what anyone would do."

"Not even close," she murmurs. And then, as if she's aware of how uncomfortable all of this has made me, she changes gears. "So, you're helping me this morning?"

I nod, beyond grateful. "How much longer do you think you have?"

She looks past me, assessing the loft. "Probably one more week or so. We're close. I've got all the paint, and I'm waiting for some things to come in that I've ordered to replace the tragedy that is your current furniture—"

"Hey!" I object.

"Except your bed. *That* is definitely staying." She grins mischievously. "I've grown awfully fond of it."

She helps me clean the dishes despite my protestations, and after, I help her lay out some drop cloths for us to paint the bathroom. She's wearing her usual tank-and-overalls outfit, her hair bound up in a light green handkerchief and her feet in steel-toed work boots. Admittedly, I'm far less prepared than she is, but the old jeans and tee I'm wearing will do just fine.

She indicates the closed can of paint. "Shake that up and get it opened and poured out, big guy, while I finish taping it off in there."

I pick the can up, then blanch. "What the hell is *mossy sun?*" I ask, reading the name of the paint color. "You better not be turning my bathroom into a damn forest, Darcy."

She giggles. "And if I were? If I had plans to paint little fairies and mushroom houses along the bottom, maybe bring in a—" She squeals as I pull her into my arms, nuzzling her neck and then tickling her bare skin inside the overalls.

"Then I'd punish you."

Her eyes sparkle as I move my hand further down her body, still inside the overalls, reaching around to cup her ass and squeeze. "But you know I like that, Mr. Hall," she breathes.

My cock stirs. I could have her pressed against the sink, buried inside her in seconds, and the temptation is almost too much to bear. I swing my hand around her thigh and palm her pussy, finding her damp with arousal. "Fuck," I groan, dropping my forehead to hers.

She breathes fast, her breath coming in little pants out of those bright red lips. I squeeze, and the moan she lets out has me almost coming in my pants.

"Painting can wait," I tell her.

Her eyes are hazy as she blinks up at me, her attention torn between the heat of my palm against her center and the words I'm speaking. "Mmm?"

I grin wickedly. "Mmm is right, baby girl. Because I'm going to let you have my cock in that pretty mouth of yours."

She snaps to attention, her eyes hyper-alert now.

I pull my hand out of her overalls. "I want fresh lipstick on those lips. And I want you naked, in my bedroom and on your knees, in three minutes."

She turns to go, and I reach for her wrist, holding it loosely as I wait for her to look back at me.

"And you know how I am about my time, Darcy Belle."

She smirks. "Yes, Daddy."

She sways away from me, heading towards her tote. I walk to the bedroom and place a pillow on the floor in front of the bed, then sit in front of it.

When exactly two minutes and fifty seconds have passed, Darcy appears in the doorway, a fucking goddess sent to torture me with visions of a forever I don't get to have.

"Did I make it in time?" She gives me a sultry smile, her lips a glossy cherry red, her body gloriously free of clothing. Her pussy is freshly trimmed, letting me see more of the pale skin beneath her dark hair. I growl in approval.

"You did."

She glances at the pillow and back to me. "You're not undressed."

I reach behind me to pull my T-shirt off, watching her expression as I go. I'll never tire of the way she looks at me, as though I'm everything she wants. And I know I'm not—I'm old and far past my prime—but there's a sick pleasure I take in knowing that I'm setting the bar really fucking high for whoever has the misfortune of coming after me. I flex my chest muscles and she grins.

"Nice." She draws the word out in obvious approval.

I bite back my own smile, then take everything else off. She watches my every move, and I let her, watching the way she bites her lip and squeezes her thighs together as her eyes land on my throbbing cock.

"You want this, Darcy?"

She nods, dragging her eyes to mine. "I do."

I take my cock in hand and give it a slow tug, more than a little pleased at the moan she gives in response. "Then get over here and show me what you can do."

She closes the distance, and it takes every ounce of my self-control to keep from throwing her onto the bed and burying my tongue in her delicious pussy.

That's not to say I don't want this. Fuck, it's been a whole other level of self-control and restraint to keep her from it. A restraint I lost for the quickest of moments when she had that beautiful ass in my face and asked for my cock, and fuck, did her mouth feel good for the short amount of time I let her have it. But letting her get me all the way off with her mouth? I've wanted to wait. More out of respect for her than anything. Guys her age are nothing but selfish pricks who rarely think about a woman's pleasure, and based on what she's told me, I'm willing to bet she's had a man's dick in her mouth far more times than she's had a tongue worshipping her pussy. Which is a damn shame.

But now, watching her chest heave as she sinks to her knees in front of me? Now's good. Now's fucking *great*.

"Wait."

She looks up at me, those ice-blue beauties all doe-eyed and innocent, despite the ways I've debauched her.

I reach for the bandana and untie it, folding it and setting it to the side. Then I gently pull her hair from the elastic binding it, sending her thick, dark hair tumbling around her shoulders. I push the hair away from her face, scraping her scalp the way she does mine, and sure enough, she closes her eyes in pleasure, a different kind of moan leaving her lips. She leans into it like a cat, all but purring as I continue to stroke her head, threading my hands through her hair as she kneels between my legs.

Finally, I stop, and she blinks up at me, something between lust and gratitude warring in her expression.

I stand, wanting to see her entire body as she kneels before me. "Put that sweet mouth on my cock, Darcy Belle."

A sinful smile spreads across her cherry red lips. "With pleasure, Daddy."

She angles forward and takes my cock in her hand. I shiver, and a low laugh issues from her as her tongue darts out to lick the pre-cum that's already formed.

"Fuck," I rasp. "You look so pretty on your knees for me."

She sucks the tip into her mouth and moans, and the sound reverberates through my entire fucking body. When her other hand reaches up to caress my balls, I nearly lose it.

She pulls her mouth away, licking around the head, her tongue pink and bright against the red lipstick. Then she opens her mouth and takes me in, wrapping those lush lips around my cock as though she's done it a thousand times. I watch as she slides her mouth back, leaving behind the faintest trace of lipstick in her wake, and I groan. "Fuck, Darcy, you're so perfect. Look at how you left your mark on me."

She hums as my dick hits the back of her throat, and I thread my hands through her hair once more. I'm trying so hard not to take over, but it's nearly impossible. Ripping my gaze from her mouth, I take in the rest of her.

"Holy shit, baby, your ass. Nothing is more perfect than your ass, except, *fuck,* your mouth. And those tits, my God." I can't stop talking, won't stop praising her, because I will never again be this lucky. I want her as long as she'll have me, and I'll want her far longer than that, but she doesn't have to know. Her head bobs as she takes me to the back of her mouth again and again, her hips flaring out to her bottom, her whole body moving in a rhythm that gets faster and faster.

It's too soon before my balls are tightening. I'm on the edge. I strengthen my grip on her hair. "I'm about to come, baby, and when I do?"

Her eyes meet mine.

"You're going to swallow every last drop."

She simply holds my gaze, then sucks.

I explode, coming with a shout and nearly blacking out, spilling down her throat like I haven't come in ages. And this beautiful woman takes it, swallowing my cum like it's everything she's ever wanted.

She pops off me and keeps going, cleaning every last bit of me with her tongue before relaxing onto the pillow, her feet tucked neatly beneath her.

I can barely keep my legs from shaking as I sit on the mattress, and the look of utter satisfaction on Darcy's face makes it all worthwhile.

"How'd I do?" she asks with a smirk.

I lean down and cup her face with both hands, pulling her to me for a kiss. "You know exactly how you did."

She laughs and flips her hair. "I do."

A laugh bursts out of me, deep and loud, and her smile grows in response. "You're amazing, Darcy Belle."

She takes the hand I offer and stands, then turns so I can palm her ass. "I know," she says over her shoulder. "It's about time you noticed."

I watch, wordless, as she sashays out of the bedroom. A minute later she calls, "Come on, big guy—this bathroom won't paint itself!"

And fuck me if she isn't everything I've ever wanted.

Chapter 20

Darcy

I'M WORKING on the finishing touches to the pool table for Anthony's loft on Sunday morning when Amanda Face-Times me.

"Hey, gorgeous," I say, propping the cell up so I can keep sanding.

"Come with me to yoga," she answers. "You know it's fun."

I frown at the phone. "Define 'fun.'"

"Come on. You owe me."

Snorting, I put down the sheet of sandpaper and look around to be sure everything is turned off and safe for me to leave it. "And what, pray tell, do I owe you for?"

She grins. "Me getting wasted enough on July Fourth that you ended up hooking up with Anthony Hall."

"You're delusional," I laugh. "But I'll see you there."

"Starts in an hour."

We're laying our mats out and Amanda waggles her eyebrows. "So…how are things going with Mr. Hall anyway?"

I sigh happily. "It's so good."

Amanda squeals with delight. "Yeah?" She leans closer and drops her voice to a whisper. "How's the sex?"

"Better than any of the guys I've been with before. By infinity." I practically swoon as I say it. "But seriously, I gotta give it to him. Maybe it's an older guy thing? But there's no drama, he's so straight-forward and he lets me know exactly where we stand." *Except for the part where I want so much more than he's willing to give.*

Suddenly the tap of nails on hardwood has me turning around, and Killer, the most adorable cream chihuahua on the planet, is making his way mat to mat as we all get settled.

"Killer!" Amanda coos with a grin. Then she points. "And there's Midnight."

The black cat haughtily surveys the space as she picks her way through the mats. The pets' owners, Goldie and Matty, and Willa and Reid, walk in behind them.

"Holy shit," I whisper, because who comes in right behind them but Anthony.

Amanda looks to the front, then back at me, a delighted smile on her face. "Now you *definitely* owe me. Did you tell him you'd be here?"

"Of course not. But I'm not mad about it."

"Yeah, you owe me."

There's no room for him to put a mat out beside me, so I keep stretching and waiting to see if he'll come over. Sure enough, he stalks over after unrolling a mat near his friends, his thigh muscles flexing with every step he takes. By the time I finish ogling his legs and raise my eyes to his, he's in front of me.

"Hi." The barest hint of a smile plays around his lips, the cocky bastard.

"Hi." Of course, I sound like a breathless toddler.

He full-on smirks, and it's sexy as hell. "Come here often?"

I swat his stomach without thinking, and he grabs it. "That's a terrible line."

Still holding my hand, he retorts, "And yet, you're still talking to me."

"Might have something to do with the fact that you're holding my hand."

A thick eyebrow raises. "And here I thought it was because I fucked you so well."

I nearly choke on my tongue as he drops my hand with a wink and returns to his mat. Beside me, Amanda laughs outright.

"Damn, that man does *not* play, does he?" she asks quietly, still grinning.

"No. No, he does not." I fan my suddenly hot face.

All throughout class, I'm distinctly aware of the stares coming my way from damn near everyone. Amanda keeps snorting every time our eyes meet, and I have no doubt that literally everyone heard what Anthony said. Willa and Goldie, in particular, seem to keep looking over, but it's not in a mean way at all, more like they're curious.

After class, we find Anthony waiting outside. I grin lazily at him, too stretched out to care that the entire yoga class knows he fucked me.

Goldie and Willa come up and introduce themselves, and I smile back. "Hi."

Reid gives us a nod and turns to Anthony. "Wanna walk with us?"

"Nah," is Anthony's response.

Willa grins at him before turning to me and Amanda. "Come by the diner sometime and let me know you're out there. Meal's on me."

"That's so sweet, thank you! I love your fries."

She grins. "It's the beef tallow, but I'm glad to hear it." She turns and tugs on Reid's arm. "Come on, Officer. Leave him alone."

"But it's so much *fun*," Reid whines, widening his eyes at Anthony as he's led away.

Matty chuckles. "See you later, man."

Amanda gives me a hug and steps away. "I gotta go, too. See you soon!"

I look at Anthony, his hazel eyes clear and amused as he gazes back. "You didn't want to go for a walk with them?"

"No."

"Do you *ever* go for walks with them?"

"No."

"Are we in one-word answer territory again?"

His lips twitch. "No."

I smile. "You're the worst."

"Come over."

"I…can't," I say with a squirm. "I want to, believe me, but I have some work to do at the shop."

"Hardware store?"

"No. *My* shop." Why is my heart racing as I say it? I blame yoga.

His eyes soften, and his voice is gentle when he speaks. "Go, then."

"You're not mad?"

He cocks his head. "Why on earth would I be mad?"

"I don't know."

"Come here," he says gruffly.

I'm not sure if it's a request or demand. I'm also not sure I care, because I do it regardless, stepping into his space and tilting my head back to look at him. He's so damn *beautiful*. Eyebrows that slash down as he stares at me, his hazel eyes flinty with what I now know isn't anger, but something more like frustrated kindness. His beard, perfectly trimmed, framing surprisingly soft and kissable lips that have brought me to orgasm more times than I can count.

He palms my hips, the wide expanse of his hands feeling more like home than ever before. "You have a life, Darcy. One that doesn't revolve around me. With passions that you should pursue without hesitation. I don't know what kind of assholes ever made you feel like you weren't able to stand on your own two feet without them, but I'm not that man."

Man. God, yes he is. I blink at him, letting the words sink in. They're a balm I didn't even know I needed. "Thank you."

"Don't thank me," he commands.

"I'm going to anyway."

"Brat."

I smile. "Maybe you can punish me later."

His eyes darken, making my heart race even faster. "Count on it."

He tips my chin up and leans down to kiss me, and I don't hesitate. A moment later, he pulls away, a satisfied smirk on his face.

"You do that a lot more now, you know."

Instantly, the smirk is replaced with a frown. "Do what?"

I hip-check him, then back away from him while grinning like a fool. "Smile."

"I don't smile," he grumbles.

"Yeah, that's a lie," I shoot back, still backing away slowly. "Because the left side of your mouth will twitch *just* a bit, and that's your version of an amused smile. But that smirk you just gave me? That's your happy smile."

His frown deepens. "Is not." But I can see him fighting a bigger smile even as he says it.

"Sure thing, Mr. Hall," I say, then twirl around to my car.

He doesn't say a thing, but when I glance back for a quick peek, he's still watching me, one hand scratching at his beard absent-mindedly.

If I didn't know any better, I'd say he might actually like me.

I swat the thought away, unwilling to let myself get lost in the fantasy. Whatever we're doing, it's temporary. How else could it be anything but that?

Chill out, Darcy, I admonish myself. It's not even been two weeks. I need to relax and let it just…be.

Even though that's so far beyond my style it's not even funny, and we all know it.

Back at my shop, I get back to the pool table. It's unlike anything I've ever seen as far as pool tables go, but to be fair, I spent precious little time looking at my competition. I watched a shitload of YouTube videos, that's for damn sure. But once I knew what I was doing, I was off and running.

Agatha appears an hour later, a glass of iced tea in her hand.

I take it with a grateful smile and put half of it away in one go. "Delicious. Thank you."

She nods and looks at the table. "It's beautiful. Who's it for?"

"Anthony." It's hard not to mumble the name, which is stupid. But suddenly I feel like a little girl with the cool older teenage sister. Which might be weird but given what I've surmised from the few stories Agatha's started to drop, I think she was pretty amazing back in the day.

And the way she's appraising me right now tells me she has a good feeling about what's going on. "Anthony Hall, huh?"

I squirm. "Yeah."

She gives a decisive nod. "Good. I like him for you. Way better than Chad, if I'm being honest."

I snort. "I was never going on a date with Chad, Agatha."

She lifts a dainty shoulder. "I promised his grandmother I'd try."

"But you—you like Anthony? For me?"

She studies me. "Girl, I have never seen you want someone's approval. What's going on?"

With a grimace, I admit, "It's just…he's older."

"And?"

I stare at her. "He's closer to my dad's age than mine."

She crosses her arms. "And?"

And, she's right. "Damn, Agatha. You're a real ball buster, you know that?"

Pointing at me, she says, "I learned from the best. Stop doing whatever you're doing. I've never seen you second-guess yourself, and I sure don't want to see you start now. Understood?"

I smile at the stern expression she wears. "Yes, ma'am."

CHAPTER 21

ANTHONY

I KNOW THAT pretty much everyone sees me as a total grump. And that's fair. But I smile like a loon when I open up the package of specially designed shirts that I had made for Darcy's bowling team.

"Hey, boss."

Harrison's voice has me shoving the shirts back into the box like I've been caught doing something wrong. Which is stupid. I own the damn bar. Hell, I own the whole damn *place*.

Ignoring my pathetic attempt to hide the shirts, Harrison continues, "Darcy told me you're not allowed up in the loft today. Also said you can't come to the front for a while, either."

I frown. "Why?"

He shrugs. "I think she's moving all the stuff in and doesn't want you to see it. Which is weird, right? Like, you approved everything—why wouldn't you be able to watch it all be moved in?"

I turn back to inventorying the bar with a grunt. The fact is, I approved exactly nothing. She asked me what colors I liked way back at the beginning, and after that, didn't ask anything else. Just barreled forward without a care in the world. I've liked the colors she's painted the walls, but hell if I know what kind of furniture and shit she's picked out.

I didn't give her any input on the furniture, either. She just… did it. Which is fine. She and I both know that I'll let her do just about anything, even though we might pretend otherwise.

"Too bad this is her last day. I've enjoyed seeing her, if you know what I mean." Harrison waggles his eyebrows suggestively.

My blood boils. "No, Harrison, I *don't* know what you mean," I say, my voice deadly calm. "Why don't you explain it just a little more?"

His eyes widen. "Dude, chill out."

"No." I can't stop the rage simmering beneath the surface. She's *mine*.

And fuck. *Fuck.* I want her. I want her for so much more than whatever this is. That's…problematic.

In front of me, Harrison's expression shifts. "Holy shit, man— you're into her."

I don't bother denying it.

His answering grin at my silence is infuriating. "That's awesome."

With a squint, I ask, "Awesome?"

He nods, then steps around me, putting some needed space between us. "Yeah. In all my years of working here, I've never seen you interested in anyone. This is great."

"Well. Okay." I don't know what else to say.

"So many things make sense now," he says, nodding to himself. "Including why you don't get to see what she's doing up there."

I rub at my chest absentmindedly. "What's she doing, exactly?"

He grins. "Oh, you'll see."

"I thought you said you didn't understand why I couldn't see it."

"I didn't. But now I do."

"You're not making any sense," I growl.

He laughs. "I'm making so much sense it's not even funny. But you can't know that yet."

"Tell me or you're fired."

Now it's a straight-up guffaw. "You're funny. Who knew you could be such a jokester?"

I turn my back on him, done with him and his shenanigans.

The day flies by. The place is hopping, a line of dads grabbing beers at the bar while their kids wreak mayhem on the machines and Skee-ball. I've already sent our high school employees to clean up spills in the party rooms and next to the claw machine, and I've been told by more than one of them that the bathrooms are under constant attack by screeching babies and toddlers.

In other words: It's a normal Thursday afternoon in late summer, during that in-between time when you've spent too much time at the beach but it's too early for dinner. And sure, it's chaotic and nearly impossible to keep things clean and up to the standards I want, but that's okay. That's kind of the fun of it, if I'm being honest. This is precisely the kind of place I'd have killed for as a kid, even if I was too poor to enjoy it more than once or twice, and I'm beyond happy to have it for the ones around now. It stings that the rest of my family doesn't see this for what it is, but it's something I have to get over.

My phone buzzes, and it's a text from Darcy.

DARCY

Ready when you are, handsome.

Biting back a smile, I send a thumbs-up. A moment later, another text comes in.

DARCY

Seriously? That's all you're giving me after two months of renovation? A thumbs-up?

Swamped down here. Another hour or so. But don't worry. When I get up there, I'm going to thank you…or punish you. 😉

DARCY

Mr. Hall, did you just send me a winking emoji? Have you been kidnapped? Send another thumbs-up if you have.

I'm tempted, but I simply click the phone off and turn back to work.

A little more than an hour later, I send an "on my way" message to Darcy and head upstairs. I find her waiting on the threshold, one of her bandanas in hand.

"Put this on," she says.

"You're cute," I answer, but I turn around and let her tie it around my eyes, anyway. It smells of her, watermelon and cherries. And out of nowhere, my heart begins to beat faster.

Sliding her hands down my arms and resting her palms on my hips, she guides me in, a tremor in her voice as she asks, "Are you excited?"

"Um, maybe?" I can't get a full breath, but I don't think it's because I'm worried about what my home will look like.

She hums. "That's fair."

A few stumbling steps later, she says I can stop. If I'm not mistaken, her hands tremble a little, too.

"Okay. You can take it off."

"You sure? You sound a little nervous," I tease.

She whacks my stomach with her hand. "Take it off."

"Yes, ma'am," I chuckle.

I pull the bandana down, and in front of me is the most gorgeous pool table I've ever seen. Sleek and yet masculine, the felt is dyed in what I can only describe as an ombre sunset. The pockets are a sumptuous woven leather the color of sand. Carved into the top edge of the table is a swirling pattern reminiscent of ocean waves, accented with bits of pearl inlay. Swallowing, I take in the woman next to me. "Darcy."

"Mm?" She looks terrified, her eyes wide, her hands fidgeting.

"Did you—did you *make* this?" My voice cracks as I speak.

She nods and clenches her hands against her sternum.

I swing my gaze back to the table. It's unlike anything I've ever seen before. It's perfect. It's exactly what I would have asked for, if I'd known something as beautiful as this could be made. My eyes sting as I turn to face her. "Darcy. No one has ever done anything like this for me before." I can't fathom what it took her to do this. The creativity. The time. The cost.

She relaxes a little, giving me a soft, nervous smile. "Do you like it?"

I take her hands in mine, feeling the callouses on them. "Darcy, I love it." *I love you.* The thought lands in my head like a sledgehammer, nearly taking me out with its intensity. I keep the words inside, pulling her into my arms and slanting my mouth over hers. Words won't do my thanks justice, so I let my mouth do the talking.

She whimpers, the sound making me go rock hard as always. Our grips tighten on each other, and I'm moving her to lean against the pool table without a second thought. I undo the overalls, palming her soft skin as they give way, then shove them down past her knees and kneel to take her boots off. When they're off, I pull the overalls off, leaving her in cotton panties and a sports bra, and she has never looked sexier.

"Does this mean you love it?" she confirms, smiling down at me.

I yank the black underwear off, then stand to sit her ass on the pool table. She yelps.

"Anthony!"

"Yes?" I answer as I kneel on the plush rug she's put beneath the table. "Nice carpet down here, by the way. Good on my knees."

"We shouldn't—"

I grin suggestively at her. "Surely you built this to be very sturdy," I admonish.

"Well, yes, but—"

"Then shut up and let me eat your pussy."

"But you haven't seen the rest—"

With one hand, I push her knees apart and lick up her seam, listening to her answering groan in return. This is, without a doubt, my favorite: hearing her pants of pleasure above me, feeling her fingers tighten in my hair and using the grip to swirl my face against her pussy as I bring her to orgasm. The fact that I have her on the custom pool table she made just for me makes it infinitely better.

She comes hard and fast, just like I want her to, and as I stand, using the back of my arm to wipe my mouth as I grin at her, she yanks me close, pulling me in for a kiss while she undoes my jeans.

"Darcy," I start.

She shoves my jeans and underwear down, then leans back on her elbows and spreads her legs. "Shut up and fuck me, Anthony."

Well. When she puts it like that.

I pull her off the table and flip her around, pressing her chest down to the felt before dropping to my knees to lick her center once again. It's only when her legs are quivering and she's begging for me that I stand and slam my cock into her, both of us shouting as I immediately start to move. She's absolutely flawless, flushed and keening, bent over a pool table I'll never use without thinking of her, and as she moans and tells me to go harder, faster, all I can think is *I love you, I love you, I love you.*

CHAPTER 22

DARCY

I SET MYSELF to rights, cleaning up and changing into the clothes I'd brought for bowling practice, and find Anthony looking at me with something very close to tenderness as I pack up my overalls. "What?"

"Nothing."

I straighten and close the distance between us. "That look isn't 'nothing.' What's going on in that head of yours?"

He gathers me to him, his big palms settling on my hips as he looks down. "Nothing." A pause. "Except, this is it, huh? No more to do up here?"

Something about the way he says it makes me hold my breath. "Anthony Hall, are you going to miss seeing me every day?"

"Yes," he says simply.

I exhale, resting my head on his chest and squeezing him. For all his bluster and carrying on, Anthony has the biggest heart of anyone I've ever known.

"Besides, who else am I going to make fun of for their taste in music?" he continues.

I laugh and pinch his side as I look up at him. "You *like* my taste in music, old man."

"Do I, though?" he asks with a wink. Then he leans down for a kiss, the simultaneously soft and rough bristles of his beard more of a comfort now than anything. He parts my lips with his tongue, the kiss quickly turning heated, and I let myself go pliant. This man can have anything he wants, anytime. I swear he could lay me out in the grocery store aisle, and I'd be down for it.

When he pulls away, he smacks my ass. "Come on, Miss Belle. You've got bowling practice to get to."

"Wait," I protest softly and take his hand, gesturing to the rest of the loft. "At least look at what I did with the place."

He smiles. *Really* smiles. "Show me around."

So, I do. I point out the extra-long, extra-deep couch and loveseat in deep gray, and the deep purple retro coffee table, tiled and kidney-shaped, that sits with them. I show him the monstera plants that require almost nothing but complement the space. The finishing touches in the bathroom and kitchen, the custom bookshelves filled with all the science fiction paperbacks I'd found in random piles around the place. In his bedroom, the lush rug in a deep sunset orange that offset the white of the duvet covering his bed. And more, each area designed to feel clean but at home, beachside but without a shell or sand-themed piece of decoration in sight.

Anthony turns to me, pulling me close and cradling my face with his hands. "Darcy. It's beautiful. Thank you."

I blink rapidly, trying to fight the tears that appear unbidden. "You probably won't thank me when you see the bill," I rasp, reaching for a joke to escape the outright tenderness I see in his expression.

"Don't do that," he admonishes gently, swiping the wetness beneath my eyes with his thumbs. "I'm trying to give you a compliment, Darcy Belle. You're astonishing, and even though you did all this without any input, you created a home that is absolutely, one hundred percent me."

And with that, he leans down and kisses me. It feels different than any kiss he's given before, infused with tenderness and care, and maybe something else that I won't dare hope for. I kiss him back, hoping he feels what I do. When he pulls away, the tension between his brows is gone, something I've never seen before.

"Thank you," I whisper.

He smiles again, and it cracks my heart wide open. "Come on. Time for bowling."

Downstairs, Anthony takes his place behind the bar, relieving Harrison and immediately making me an Aperol Spritz. He slides it in front of me and I raise a brow.

"Who said this was what I wanted?"

He smirks. "You're wearing orange."

I glance down at the shirt, which does, in fact, have a bit of orange in it. "So?"

He leans his elbows onto the bar, self-satisfaction oozing from him. "I've figured you out, my dear. You choose your drinks to match your clothes."

I catch my breath. *My dear.* "I most certainly do not," I counter.

For the third time in half an hour, he smiles. A real, actual smile—in *public*. I half want to look around to see if I'm being pranked. Then he says, "You may not realize it, but you do."

"Okay, well, I'd planned on ordering an Aperol Spritz anyway, so that was just a good guess by you." Why am I so flustered? He can't know me that well...can he?

But then I think back over the past few months. The way he could make my coffee after one day. The way a silk pillowcase appeared on one of his pillows the first night I slept over. How he knows precisely where to touch me, where to graze his teeth and where to bite, how hard I like to be spanked, the angle that'll make me moan like nothing else. My favorite kind of pen, even.

I don't get a chance to investigate how all this really makes me feel before the rest of the crew wanders in, none of them surprised to see me already at the bar, drink in hand.

Anthony has each woman's drink ready to go, but before we turn to the lane, he stops us.

"I have something for you."

They all look at me, but I lift my shoulders. "No idea," I say, my own curiosity just as piqued. "What's going on?"

He reaches for something beneath the bar, then pulls out four different gift bags.

"Did you get us presents?" Agatha asks.

"Unless this is his new way of presenting a bill," Devon jokes, "then yes, Agatha, I'm willing to bet these are gifts."

Amanda's dark eyes flash to mine, certain I have an answer, but I'm just as clueless as the rest of them. Shaking my head at her, I take a bag from Anthony. "What's this?"

But he says nothing, just crosses his arms and nods brusquely at us.

"That's Anthony-speak for 'open them,'" I joke. I pull open the bag—no tissue paper to remove, it's just the bag, but honestly, it's still impressive considering the man who's put this together—and pull out a shirt.

I gasp. Not just a shirt—a *bowling* shirt. Styled in a retro design from the fifties, it boasts thick pink and white stripes, with little red cherries on the front pockets that are actually bowling balls when I look closer. My name is stitched in black beneath the cherry bowling balls, and on the back, in black script, are the words *Hall's Belles*.

My throat constricts, and I blink up in time to catch yet another soft look on his face. He meets my eyes as I mouth, "thank you," right as the other women begin to squeal and say their thanks.

And the way his mouth tips up just the slightest, his hazel eyes crinkling so minutely that I swear I'm the only one who can tell? *Ugh*. Be still my beating heart. Because this is the final proof that he cares. Maybe a lot more than he's ever let on.

"These are amazing," I croak.

"What's with the name?" Amanda asks. "Who says we're Hall's Belles?"

"Awfully presumptuous of you," Devon teases.

He grunts. "I've heard you referring to yourselves as that, and besides, that's what you're signed up to compete as."

"Why, Anthony Hall, did you actually look us up?" Agatha's eyes shine bright as she sizes him up.

His cheeks get the barest shade of pink above his beard. It's so subtle that I'm not sure anyone notices. "Of course."

The women howl.

"All of you still need to work on your approach," he says next.

"Let me guess." I carefully place the shirt back in its bag and inject a snarky tone into my words, if only to keep up a farce I'm not even sure is needed. "You're going to be our coach?"

He tilts his head and regards me silently, then gestures Harrison back over from where he'd been cleaning up the pool area. He walks to our reserved lane, and we follow. Producing a key, he opens a compartment beneath the benches and pulls out bowling shoes and the same customized ball he used the last time he came over.

"You're getting better," he finally says, "but you all still need a lot of work. And now that my name is on your shirts, you need to step it up."

After we're all in our bowling shoes, Anthony instructs us to watch as he gets into position, pulling the ball up to his chin like he's a baseball pitcher and the ball is his mitt.

"He really *does* have a nice ass," Amanda murmurs, a playful smirk on her lips.

Devon snorts as I lean into Amanda and shush her, all of us paying attention to Anthony's, um, *form.*

He takes four quick steps, pulling his right arm back with the ball, and then, on his final approach, swings his right leg back as his arm levers forward, releasing the ball perfectly down the center. It lands with a satisfying *thwack* a good third of the way into the lane, swooshing down without even seeming to roll, before finally beginning to spin on a collision course with the front pin. One second later, the ball hits the pink in a beautiful nose hit, sending it crashing into the others. It's a strike.

Everyone cheers while I try not to be as turned on as I am. It's just bowling, for God's sake. But…damn, did he look hot.

He pivots to face us. "Ready to learn how to do that?"

Chapter 23

Darcy

IT TURNS OUT that Anthony is a freaking *beast* at bowling. Surprising everyone, honestly. Why the man never truly bothered to mention it other than the first time he showed off for us is a mystery, but with only one week to go, he took it upon himself to put our team through its paces, making us come to Hall's Balls every night to practice.

Then, after wringing us out night after night, he'd take me upstairs and we tumbled into bed. It's been the best week of my life, but also the most intense and most stressful.

Last night, Anthony pulled us all together and gave us what was, I'm sure in his mind, a very inspiring pep talk. But the man is no Ted Lasso, or even Coach Saban. I'm honestly not sure what he said because I blacked out imagining him using the same voice on me as he made me swallow his cock, so when Amanda snorted while simultaneously saying "Thanks, Anthony," all I could do was nod.

And if you're wondering, I absolutely asked him to use that same voice on me last night…while coaching me to, well, swallow his cock like a good girl.

I wave my suddenly heated face in the morning breeze of

Mobile, the location of the bowling tournament, and take a giant slurp of the extra-large iced coffee with vanilla cold cream that Amanda, God bless her soul, handed to me wordlessly when I climbed into her car this morning. Agatha carpooled with us, but she had her thermos of sweet iced tea and wanted nothing to do with our "overpriced coffee shenanigans."

Devon showed up with Aaron, and Agatha's daughter Betty is also here.

"Hey, Darcy girl," comes my dad's gruff voice as he wraps an arm around me and pulls me to him.

"Dad!" I look up in surprise. "You're here?"

He winks down at me. "Wouldn't miss it."

I tip up to kiss him on his leathery cheek. "Thank you. Means a lot." And it does, more than I thought it would, judging by the way my heart ka-thumps in happiness. It's the first time he's shown up for me like this, but in fairness, it's the first time in my life I've done anything approaching sporty. "Can't believe it's finally here!" I gush, looking at the bowling pin sign that turns slowly in the air above us.

"*I* can't believe we all got here on time," Amanda snorts.

"With everything we needed," Agatha adds.

"In our shirts!" Devon finishes.

I laugh. "C'mon, ladies. Let's go register and see if we can intimidate our competition with our sweet matching shirts."

A half hour later, an announcer calls the raucous room to attention. "Each bowler rolls ten frames, and the team with the highest score wins. We have thirty teams here, so we're breaking you into six sets of five. The top three teams in each set of five will move on to the next round, meaning we'll have eighteen teams remaining. From there, we'll break you into six sets of three, and the top two teams in each will progress, getting us to twelve teams. We'll take a break, then after that, the twelve teams break into six sets of two. The highest-scoring six teams will then bowl against each other. The top three teams go on for the final placement. Questions?"

No one dares raise a hand. Pretty sure the woman barking instructions at all of us scared just about the entire room.

Ignoring my ridiculous wish that Anthony could be here—my dad is here, and Anthony has a whole business to run, and it feels like I'm being greedy—I turn to my team and grin. "Let's go, girls!"

"Woo, a Shania Twain reference!" comes Agatha's enthusiastic hoot.

I'm gonna be honest: my only goal was to get us all here and bowling. Imagine my surprise when we actually make it through the first cut—*and* we're not even at the very bottom. That distinction falls to the group of middle school teenage girls who look like they're trying to make bowling the modern version of the word "fetch." In other words, it's not going great. But alllll the points for enthusiasm.

"Looks like you made it to the next round."

I turn, surprised at the gravelly voice behind me. "Anthony?"

His hazel eyes bright, he tips a grin at me. "Did you think I wouldn't come?"

"I mean…a little," I admit. "You're busy."

He tilts his head and frowns. "Darcy. Of course I'd come. This is your moment!" Then he steps closer and murmurs, "Plus, I worked my ass off with you four this past week. I deserve to see some action."

I giggle. "You're insane." Still, there's no denying the way my insides warm at his actions. He pulls me to him, and I wrap my arms around his neck, tipping up to kiss him. The distinctive woodsy-Anthony scent of him curls around me. "Thank you," I whisper.

His hands are warm and reassuring on my waist. "Any time." He steps away and claps. "Okay, girls, let's kick some ass."

Agatha howls again, making all of us laugh. "You got it, Coach."

"Give me the rundown, Amanda," he says.

Amanda's cheeks blaze, but she does it, pointing out who we're up against and what she's seen from each team. When she's done, I gawk at her.

"What?" she asks self-consciously.

"You—holy shit, Amanda, you know your stuff!"

She shrugs, her blush deepening. "I mean...yeah."

I shake my head. "I'm so impressed with you right now I could kiss you."

She's saved from my affections by all of us being called to start the next set. We're in the first heat of nine teams and our lane is dead center.

Anthony sucks his teeth. "Not great positioning, but that's okay." He takes off at a business-like stride, and the four of us look at each other, shrug, and follow.

After a game in which I was almost certain we were on fire we were playing so well, we break for the next set of nine. Nearly an hour later, we learn that we've made it into the next bracket of twelve.

Which is unbelievable.

But what's even more wild is that we get to the top six.

At this point, I'm in full-body chills. No way is this even happening. Like, we're four random ladies—three of whom I essentially bullied into doing this—and yet, we've held our own in our very first tournament!

"Huddle up," Anthony says. We gather around, and he lays out the strategy. Which isn't ground-breaking: the strategy is to play our hearts out.

That's it.

Play.

Seems easy enough. Or hard enough, depending on how you look at it. But no matter, because we head out and take our place at the third lane from center, which Anthony had been angling for us to have the entire time. Something about the oil sheen looking the best out of all the lanes.

And so, with my dad, Devon's husband Aaron, and Agatha's daughter Betty cheering us on from the side, we do exactly what Anthony asked us to do: we play our hearts out.

It's not enough to take first, second, or even third. But our fourth-place statue is the greatest thing I think I've ever achieved in my adult life, and we take way too many pictures with it. I'm pretty sure we were more excited about our fourth-place finish than the winners were with their giant trophy. After packing up our shoes and balls, I hear my name.

"Darcy." Dad's face is drawn and pensive.

I frown. "Dad?"

"A word? Outside?"

"I—sure?" I look at the group, and everyone is still celebrating, laughing and smiling and carrying on. Even Anthony is almost smiling, off to the side and talking to Aaron.

I follow Dad outside, and we're barely out of the door before he whirls on me. "What is that in there?"

I draw up short. "Excuse me?"

"You and Anthony. Did you think I didn't see the way you two hugged and kissed?" He says the last word as though it pains him.

And for the first time in my life, I'm actually speechless.

Dad does not have that problem, however, because he keeps going. "Do you have any idea how old he is? How old he was when you were *born*? What in the world do you think you're doing? You're a—"

"I'm a what, Dad?" I finally say, my voice having come roaring back alongside my temper. "Because I'll tell you exactly what I am: a grown woman who can do what she wants, when she wants, and *who* she wants."

He winces, but it doesn't stop him. "It's disgusting, Darcy."

My head whips back so quickly that it feels like I give myself whiplash. "Disgusting?" My voice cracks. "You know absolutely nothing about it."

He crosses his arms. "Well, maybe disgusting is a strong word—"

"It's a terrible word, Dad," I interrupt.

"He's too old for you, Darcy."

"I'm a grown woman, Dad," I shoot back. "I don't know what it'll take to get you to see that, but I am. And this isn't the nineteen-fifties—you don't have any say in this."

My words don't seem to faze him. "Do you love him? Because no way does he love you." His tone is gentle, soft even, as though he's delivering a killing blow but still feels bad about it.

And it hurts. God, does it hurt. All of it. His unkind words, the seeds of doubt he's planted…all of it. Crossing a hand over my stomach in a bid to keep myself from doubling over, I swallow the lump in my throat. "Thanks for your concern."

His eyes are kind. "I'm just worried about you, Darcy. You're my little girl."

I shake my head, resolved. "But I'm not. Whether this thing with Anthony goes the distance or not, I'm *not* your little girl. I stopped being that a long time ago, even though you never wanted to see it."

He blows out a breath, bringing his gaze to mine once more. "Be careful on the way home." Without another glance, he walks away.

I will not cry. I will not cry. I will not cry. I keep repeating it over and over until Dad is out of sight.

And because life is a fickle bitch, all my friends come out right then, still happy and hollering about winning.

Anthony's arm wraps around me, hugging me to his side as he looks around for my dad. "Jim have to go?"

I nod silently, unable to say anything.

"Want a ride?"

Again, I nod, grateful for the layer of numbness that's washed over me. But I smile and hand out hugs and excited squeals to everyone else, keeping it together until Anthony opens his truck door for me.

I pull myself into the cab, Anthony gently shutting the door behind me with a concerned look sweeping across his face. It undoes me, and I cry, trails of silent tears streaking down my cheeks. Which pisses me off. I'm not a crier. Unless I've really hurt myself, but crying over something emotional isn't my bag.

Not until now, apparently.

Anthony starts the engine and places a warm palm on my knee. He doesn't ask what's wrong, just reverses out of the parking lot and gets onto the road. The unspoken acceptance releases something in me, and I sob, covering my face with my hands, shoulders shaking. Anthony's palm remains on my leg, his thumb moving back and forth over the fabric of my skirt, and I let it all out.

It isn't until we're ten minutes onto the highway, another twenty to go, when I finally stop crying and clean my face with the tissues in his glove compartment.

Quietly, Anthony asks, "Do you want to talk about it?"

I sniffle. "Yes."

"Then lay it on me, baby."

"Dad said that you and I were..." I can't bring myself to say the word, especially because I'm not really sure Dad meant it to be as cruel as it was. Maybe that makes me naive, but I can't believe he truly meant to be as hurtful as he was. "He isn't a fan of this." I settle on the easiest way to put it, gesturing between the two of us.

"Understandable." He seems so calm and relaxed. Like he just accepts that my dad might hate him. One hand on the steering wheel, the other still resting on my upper thigh like it has every right to be there.

I tense. "Seriously?"

Anthony chuffs. "He's your dad. He's not going to be a fan of anyone who dates his daughter. And when it's some old geezer who's probably closer to his age than his daughter's?"

I stiffen. "It's not his business," I say, leaning into the anger.

"It's not," he agrees.

"And did he really have to say something today? After what was supposed to be a really happy time? Like, shit. I've never won anything, Anthony. Ever. I finally do it with a team of women I love, and the first thing my dad does is shit all over my day with a speech about I'm too young? Fuck that."

"Darcy."

"No. Stop it with the placating tone. It was totally uncalled for. And why aren't you mad? You get mad at everything."

He chuckles. "I don't get mad at everything. I just frown a lot. And I don't talk. Not my fault that people assume I'm mad."

My chest is tight. The air conditioner can't fight the flush on my cheeks. "You're not helping."

He puts his blinker on, then guides us to the side of the interstate and slowly comes to a stop. Cars whoosh by, rocking the truck as they do.

"What are you doing?"

Putting the truck in park, he turns to look at me. "What do you want from me, Darcy?"

"What do you mean?" My emotions swirl, unable to land on anything.

"Do you want sympathy, or do you want solutions? An ear, or actions? Tell me what you want, and I'll give it to you."

"I want you to be just as pissed off and confused as me!" My words come out forcefully, and they take me aback.

But not Anthony. He nods, licking his lips and studying me intently.

I take a deep breath and let it out. "How aren't you mad?"

A sympathetic grin. "Because I see his side of it. And I see yours. Beauty of being forty-one, I guess. Nothing is black and white."

"Yeah, well, tell that to Jim Belle," I snark, crossing my arms and wanting nothing more than to wallow in petulance. Seems like a great place to be right now.

"I will, if you want me to."

"Ugh, stop being so understanding!" I groan in frustration.

He leans over, cupping my chin and pulling me to him for a soft kiss. He deepens it instantly, sweeping his tongue into my mouth and claiming me with a sureness that I'm desperate for. I kiss him back, needy and eager, but this time it's not a physical need. It's emotional. And it wallops me so hard that it nearly takes my breath away.

Even still, the kiss doesn't settle me. It might actually make it worse, because all I want to do is go to the hardware store and yell at my dad that if he'd just give me one ounce of understanding like the incredible man driving this truck, he'd see I'm happier than I've ever been.

He'd see that I love this man.

The realization is unsettling. Terrifying, actually. Am I deciding I love him purely out of spite? Or has it taken something like this to push me to that realization?

I don't know.

"Darcy, I..." he stops, his eyes searching mine.

For one heart-stopping moment, I think he's going to say the very words I just thought. *I love you.*

But he doesn't. Instead, he sighs. "I'm on your side. Always. Okay?"

I nod silently, not trusting myself to speak.

The gravel crunches beneath the tires as Anthony pulls us back onto the highway, the engine revving as we get back up to speed.

"I know what I need." The words come out steady.

Anthony simply glances at me, nothing but understanding in his eyes.

"Take me home. I need power tools."

"Hell yeah, you do." He grins, then punches the gas.

CHAPTER 24

ANTHONY

I HATE WAKING up alone. I hate going to bed alone. I hate making a small pot of coffee. I hate taking a shower by myself and seeing the shampoo and conditioner that isn't mine sitting in the shower, taunting me.

I hate that I'm too busy to go to my spot on the beach and sit and think. I hate the snot-nosed little kids that are running around like hooligans and absolutely refuse to listen to me when I tell them not to run, because their parents sure as shit can't be bothered to do it.

I want Darcy. I want to wake up with her. I want her teasing me. I want everything about her, always. But I sure as shit haven't figured out a way to tell her. I need to—hell, I *want* to, but she retreated like a turtle after the blow-up with her dad yesterday. I dropped her off at her house as requested, then came back to work to focus on anything that wasn't Darcy. The problem was that everything I saw reminded me of her. The bowling lanes, obviously. Pool tables that didn't hold a candle to the masterpiece she'd hand-crafted for me upstairs. The drinks I made, each one somehow tying back to her. And I slept like shit, grabbing the silk pillow next to me and breathing in her scent, which only got me hard instead of helping me drift off to sleep.

I'm a fucking wreck.

I don't like seeing her sad. But I can't fix that. It's not my place, and if I want any kind of lasting thing with her, then I sure as shit don't need to stick my nose into her and her dad's relationship.

Should I text her? I should.

I dump the empty glasses into the bin behind the bar and whip my phone out before I can overthink it.

> Good morning, gorgeous.

She doesn't respond, but I know that Sundays are the one day she lets herself sleep in. If it were any other Sunday, I'd have slept in with her, then I'd have woken her by worshipping her body with my mouth. I'd have left this chaos to Harrison.

Harrison, who I'm realizing has been quietly taking on more and more responsibility around here.

The kid himself appears in my periphery, standing and talking with a parent outside of one of the party rooms. He finishes with a nod and a business-like smile, then turns my way.

His smile fades as he nears me. "What did I do?"

"Nothing."

"Then why are you looking at me like that?"

"Like what?"

"Like that."

"I'm just looking."

He squints. "Yeah, but you might be kind of...smiling? I don't know. But you're freaking me out, man. Is Darcy making you *nice*?"

"How long have you been working here?"

His brow furrows. "Ten years. You know I started here when I was sixteen, right?"

I consider it. "Damn."

He laughs. "I have a degree in business, Anthony."

"Then what the fuck are you doing here?" I counter.

"Seriously? You need someone looking out for your grumpy ass. And who else is going to do all the shit around here that needs doing for the pittance you pay me?"

"You need a raise."

He grins. "Of course I do. You should double my salary."

I scoff. "Don't get ahead of yourself."

He leaves, and sure as shit, I spend the next few hours wondering what in the hell I'm actually doing. With myself. With Darcy. Hell, even Harrison.

Seems I've had my head stuck all the way up my ass for quite some time, but no one was bothering to say anything. Or maybe they were, and I just wasn't hearing it. Either way, I need to fucking focus.

Harrison's the easiest. The guy really does need a raise and title change, because he runs way more of this place than I've bothered to realize. It's definitely not me talking to the parents, that's for sure. Hell, I'm willing to bet that anyone who doesn't live here probably thinks that Harrison is the owner. So, fine. Done. I make a note to pull him to the side and talk with him about it all soon. Today is insane.

Darcy. Darcy, Darcy, Darcy. Wiping the bar after a patron throws cash on it and runs after a kid, I still don't quite know what to do.

I love her.

But is that enough? I truly don't know. It should be, but…

Fuck. I don't know. It's frustrating.

"What's got you looking so down in the dumps?"

With a jerk of my head, I make eye contact with my brother. "Ox."

He smirks. "I should make you call me Chief."

"The fuck you will," I grumble.

He laughs. "You started making plans for the celebration?"

"No."

"Of course you haven't. You need to at least make sure Harrison knows."

"Knows what?" Harrison appears at the end of the bar.

"About our parents' wedding anniversary-slash-Dad's-retirement-party that we're having."

His head swivels to me. "And you didn't think to mention this?"

I shrug. "Haven't gotten around to it."

His jaw ticks.

Ox laughs. "It's August 25th."

Immediately, Harrison pulls the iPad open and consults it, then heaves a sigh of relief. "We're good. Nothing's booked."

"We're not having it here," I bark.

Harrison raises an eyebrow at me. "Okay."

With a glare at Ox, I say, "Which is why it wasn't a big deal that I mention it to you."

"Oh, I don't know," he muses, rubbing his chin, "You not being here all day *is* something I'd need to know."

I roll my eyes. "I admit that you do a bunch more around here than I give you credit for, and suddenly you're giving me attitude?"

He grumbles something under his breath, then leaves.

Ox watches him go, then turns back to me. "Okay, spill it. What's going on?"

"Nothing."

"Bullshit. You're mopeyer than usual."

"That's not a word."

"You know what I mean, asshole. Answer the question."

"I liked it better when I could put you in a headlock." I tilt my head, considering. "I bet I still could."

Ox crosses his arms and glares at me. "And I bet I'd arrest you for assaulting a police officer."

"It might be worth it."

He chuckles. "Seriously. What the hell is wrong with you?"

"Nothing you can help me with."

Ox wedges himself against the bar, leaning onto his elbows and getting as close to me as possible. "Anthony. Quit being a grumpy-ass grump and tell me what's wrong. You should know that I'm like a dog with a bone, man. Tell me."

I walk away to serve a customer, and my brother, persistent asswipe that he is, stays exactly where he is, waiting patiently. Fucking cops. Fucking *brothers*. Fucking brothers who are cops.

"You like her. No—you *love* her," Ox declares when I finally make my way back to him.

I stare.

He grins. "Knew it."

CHAPTER 25

DARCY

MY BODY ACHES. Both from the massive walk I took along the beach yesterday and the tournament the day before.

My heart aches, too.

I look down at yesterday's text exchange with Anthony.

ANTHONY

Good morning, gorgeous

> Just home from a long walk on the beach. It's beautiful today.

ANTHONY

How are you?

> I'm okay. Had a lot on my mind.

ANTHONY

Want to talk about it?

> No but thank you. Talk tomorrow?

ANTHONY

Of course. Come over if you change your mind.

I hadn't changed my mind. I spent all day yesterday thinking. And thinking a little more. I've made some hard decisions, but they're exciting all the same.

Now that the job at Anthony's is done, I'd normally head into the hardware shop, ready to tackle whatever it is that Dad left undone over the past day, or week, or even month. The man needs a keeper.

The thing is…I'm not going to be the one to do it.

With my iced coffee half-downed in preparation, I fling myself onto the couch, grab a doily for good luck, and dial.

"You still mad at me?" Dad asks when he answers.

"No," I sigh softly. "Not that you don't deserve it."

His voice tight, Dad answers, "You're right. I'm…I'm sorry, Darcy girl. But—"

"No," I interrupt him. "You can't say 'I'm sorry *but*.' That's right up there with telling someone you're sorry if you offended them. You're either sorry or you're not."

He's silent for a beat. "You sound just like your mother sometimes," he says wistfully. "I mean that in a good way, too. She was just as strong as you. You're smarter. Hell," he chuckles, "you're smarter than the both of us ever hoped to be."

My heart squeezes at his words. She died when I was too young to remember her, but it's always been clear that Dad loved her. "Thanks, Dad."

"I'm sorry. Truly."

"No 'but'?"

Huffing out a laugh, he confirms, "No 'but.' I remain concerned—"

"Dad," I warn.

"*And* it's only the regular amount of concern a father has about his daughter. Which is a lot. It's not Anthony-specific."

I take a fortifying sip of my coffee. "Good."

"You coming in?"

Blowing out a breath, I answer. "That's the other reason I'm calling."

"Sounds ominous."

"Depends on your perspective, I suppose," I hedge.

"Well, then, spit it out."

"I'm, um, I'm opening my own shop." The instant the words are out, I feel lighter.

"In town?" Dad asks, nothing but curiosity in his tone.

"No," I laugh. "Online."

"What are you selling?"

Part of me is crushed by the question. The other part of me knows that Dad means it in the nicest, sweetest way. But has the man paid no attention? Or—the thought crashes into me—have I ever bothered telling him?

"Darcy girl?" he prompts.

"Little bit of this and a little bit of that," I answer. "Tables, dressers, custom pool tables. That sort of thing."

"Well now, that sounds like a big job. How are you going to fit it in with working here?"

It hits me, then, what a coward I'm being by having this conversation over the phone. But it's done, so there's nothing to do but keep going. I reach for the spark of irritation that flared the second he assumed I would fit *my* dream into *his* world and rip off the metaphorical bandage. "I'm not going to work full-time at the hardware store, Dad. Effective immediately."

He sucks in a breath, and for several moments, he's quiet. When he finally speaks, it's to utter one simple word: "Oh."

I swallow. "So, that's that." I throw the doily over my face and stare at the ceiling through its lacy holes.

We make a little more stilted conversation after that, but I'm antsy and need to do something with my hands, and Dad must sense it, because he lets me go.

I practically run to the garage to find something to do, and after an hour of zoning out to the precision of woodwork, my shoulders finally relax. And a half-hour after that, I'm sitting at the tiny kitchen table, staring at the tiny little button that'll turn my new website on.

With a click, it's on, and I exhale, shaking my hands to expel the nervous energy that's built right back up. But I keep going, navigating over to Instagram to make my first post with shots of Anthony's pool table, then scheduling reels that show my progression on it, to demonstrate how I work.

What I learned while making the pool table is how hard it is to take something as well-known as a pool table and create something new. That level of creativity and problem-solving was new for me, and I *loved* it. It felt purposeful. As though engaging in the creation of something beautiful was worthwhile. Worthy of my time. And by extension, it made *me* feel worthy. Something that I didn't know I was even looking for.

I thought I was perfectly content working at the hardware store and moonlighting as a carpenter, but renovating Anthony's loft and making that pool table was nothing short of revolutionary for me. I'll always be a carpenter, and I'll always help Dad when he needs it—but this, officially opening myself up to custom orders from people around the world and not relying on the few orders I've had by word of mouth? *This* is what I'm meant to do.

Speaking of Anthony.

With a grin, I take a shower and head his way.

I PIT STOP AT THE DASH IN DINER FIRST, AND OF course I'm greeted by Tom and Jerry on their customary stools on the far end of the counter. Willa nods and smiles at me from the kitchen window, and I make my order with a teenager who looks like she's one minute away from collapsing in a heap of tears.

"You okay?" I lean forward and ask.

She gives me a watery look. "Yeah, just trying to keep a straight face around those two."

I look where she indicates. "Tom and Jerry?"

She sniffs and nods. "They're hilarious, but I made a bet with Miss Willa that I wouldn't laugh."

That, of course, makes *me* laugh, but I clap my hand over my mouth to spare the girl.

Before long, I'm making my way up the back stairs that I spent way too long restoring and let myself in with the spare key that Anthony rolled his eyes about me having.

"Of course you can have a key," he'd said. *"Even if I said no, you'd probably produce some crazy skeleton key like the hardware store kid you are."*

He might be right. But I'll never tell him.

The scent of his shower gel hits me when I let myself in, and I grin. By the time he's come out, striding nearly naked across the loft like he always does—and God, I hope he never stops—I've plated dinner at the new farm-style table, complete with deep red napkins and new silverware, and am scrounging around for wine glasses to go with the bottle I impulse-bought on the way here.

I feel very grown up.

Which is silly. I'm twenty-four, so of *course* I'm grown up. But I don't know. It feels like today I'm making some major Big Girl Steps, and it feels so damn good.

"Darcy?"

My mouth goes dry at the sight of him, water droplets snaking down his bare torso, a thin towel wrapped loosely around his waist. When I meet his eyes, I'm confronted with a mixture of hope and wariness. I try to infuse as much warmth as possible in my smile when I say, "I brought dinner."

"Guess I should get dressed, then," he offers.

I shrug and let my gaze wander over his impressive body. "I'll never tell you to put clothes on, Mr. Hall."

His lips quirk up the tiniest bit.

A few minutes later, I've got the wine poured just as Anthony emerges from the bedroom. He's in gray sweatpants—which I've told him are criminally distracting—and a plain black T-shirt, his bare feet padding across the loft as he nears the table.

"This is nice," he says, then pins his eyes to mine as we each take a seat. He holds his wine glass aloft, then murmurs a quiet, "Thank you."

We drink.

"I missed you," I confess as I place my glass on the table. "But I needed the alone time, if that makes sense."

He hums, cutting into his salad and taking a bite. His shoulders are relaxed, and there's no tension in the set of his jaw. All signs that I've learned are him giving me the space I need to work out what I need to say. And whether that's a product of him being seventeen years older than me or not, I appreciate it. Something tells me he's always been like this: patient, giving.

I love you. Everything in me screams to say it, but for all my supposed growth over the past couple of days, I take the easy way out. "I launched my website and posted my first content."

His eyes light up. "For your business?"

I nod, my expression matching his.

"Darcy, that's incredible. I'm so fucking proud of you. How do you feel?"

And see, that right there? That's what I'm talking about. "Like I love you." My hand slaps over my mouth, and my eyes are probably the size of headlights. I literally just thought I was too scared to say something, but then he tells me he's proud of me and thinks to ask how I feel, and I'm blurting it out without a second thought.

But the smile that spreads across his face, bright and beautiful and so fucking *sexy* it hurts, helps me breathe a little easier. "I love you, too."

"You do?" I squeak, my hand still over my mouth.

"Yeah, baby, I do." He stands and tosses his napkin to the table, then holds his hand out. "Dinner can wait. Come here."

I place my fingers in his palm, and he encircles them with his own. Wordlessly, I rise, my own napkin falling to the floor as he pulls me gently to his bedroom.

As we cross the threshold, my heart thrums, caught between wanting to take flight and wanting to burrow into Anthony's body and make itself at home there. The way he looks at me… holy shit. He lifts his hands, then cups my chin, tipping it up to his mouth and capturing my lips with his. His beard scrapes my skin, and I relish the feel.

I wrap my hands around his waist, guiding them beneath his shirt to roam across the expanse of his skin, the feel of coarse hair tickling my palms, the sound of his sharp inhale as I gently pinch his nipples. "I need your skin," I murmur.

He obeys, pulling his shirt off and then going for mine, the two of us tugging it off simultaneously. His hands thread through my hair, pushing it away from my face and down my back. "This hair of yours," he whispers. "Do you know how I fantasized about it? Wanted so badly to see it down, to feel it between my fingers? So fucking soft and silky." He nuzzles my neck, and I go on my tiptoes to give him better access, releasing a gasp as his teeth graze my ear.

His hands roam farther, rounding my ass and squeezing before tucking his thumbs into the skirt and pushing it down my thighs. "And this skirt. Jesus, woman—did you wear this on purpose?"

I moan as his lips find the tender flesh of my breast and suck, holding him in place. I want the mark, want to be branded by him. "I did," I admit, digging my nails into his hair and scraping his scalp just like he loves.

He groans, dipping as his knees bend to pull the skirt the rest of the way off. He divests me of my shoes, then straightens, hissing as I grab for his dick through the sweatpants. "Did *you* wear these on purpose?"

His answering chuckle is dark and knowing. "Of course I did. Now lay on the bed and let me look at you."

I obey, not interested in being punished this evening. Only worshipped.

"Every curve is so fucking sexy," he says, his bobbing cock providing irrefutable proof.

"Touch yourself," I whisper.

He smirks. "Dip your finger into that pussy and show Daddy how wet you are."

I squirm. "Fuck, that's hot." I don't hesitate, pushing a finger through my folds and displaying my arousal for his inspection.

"Lick it off, sweetheart."

I give him the show he wants, raising my finger to my mouth and sucking it in, closing my eyes to clean it and releasing with a pop.

"Good girl," he praises, fisting his cock and giving it a slow pump. "You gonna take them off for me? Let me see that glistening pussy?"

I start with my bra, then move to the lacy panties, and when I spread my legs for his perusal, my core goes absolutely molten at the way his eyes darken to a forest green with lust. I squirm again, needing relief, and he notices.

"Tell me what you want, Darcy Belle." His voice is dark with promise. "I'll give it to you."

"Say it again." I need to hear it.

He climbs onto the bed, crawling over me with the grace of a dancer and lowering himself between my legs. His cock lays heavy on my abdomen, and he thrusts against my core slowly, giving me the pressure I'm so desperate for. Our eyes don't leave each other as he repeats, "I love you, Darcy."

I exhale, squeezing my eyes shut with relief for a brief

moment, and when I open them, it's to see him studying me with an intensity I'm not sure I've ever seen out of him. "I love you, Anthony."

He kisses me then, and in seconds, he's positioning his cock to push into me, the both of us gasping for air around the kiss. He feels different, somehow. Bigger, filling me even more than before. And when we come together, his release spilling inside of me, I hold him to me, unwilling to let him move.

CHAPTER 26

ANTHONY

IS THIS WHAT normal people feel all the time? This… peace? I think that's what it is. *This* is what I've missed all these years? All because of one woman. A woman I am head over heels for.

Yeah, this is good shit. I'll take it. I'll take it all damn day.

The past two weeks have been amazing. I've seen Darcy almost every night, sometimes with her at my place, and sometimes me visiting her tiny cottage, spending time in the workshop and watching her work. She's already gotten an order for a pool table from some fancy celebrity in California, and the way she lit up when she told me about it…that might have been one of the best feelings in the world. If she's happy, I'm happy.

Tonight is bowling team night, and Darcy's been at her place working on the pool table order most of the day. I don't see her until she struts in, sporting the Hall's Balls shirt as her hips swaying beneath yet another form-fitting red skirt that makes my mouth water. The shirt is tied just above the waistline of her skirt, revealing a tantalizing strip of skin every time she moves. Her hair is done up in some kind of curled ponytail thing, glossy and bouncy, and those velvet red lips curve into a smile when she sees me.

I slide the cocktail across the bar in greeting.

She looks down at it, considering. "It's a Paloma."

"Vodka, not tequila," I clarify.

"Because your beloved does not, in fact, like tequila."

I wink at her, then turn to make the other women's drinks as they enter. Soon enough, they're off bowling, and Aaron tips his beer at me. "You look different."

I shrug. "Maybe."

He laughs. "Things are going well with Darcy, then?"

"You know about us?"

He laughs harder. "C'mon, man, you think they don't talk? Of course I know about you two."

Something inside my chest unfurls and loosens, and I gotta say, it feels great. "Yeah, it's going well."

He toasts me, then takes another swig.

Out of the corner of my eye, I see a swath of dark blue, followed by my brother and his wife. "Shit," I mutter.

Aaron's eyes narrow, and when he swivels to see what's got me scowling, all he does is snort a laugh into his beer. "Judging by your expression, that's gotta be your other brother."

"I'm not sure I like you," I quip, then cross my arms and turn to my brothers and Charlotte.

"Anthony," Levi says.

"Levi," I answer.

"Look at the love!" Ox enthuses. "It just oozes from their pores, don't you think, Charlotte?"

Charlotte's grin is knowing. "Definitely."

I decide there's no point in being an ass to Charlotte. I like her, and she's been good for my brother. Instead of him being an asshole one hundred percent of the time, it's more like eighty percent. And that's not nothing.

Is he an asshole because I was one first? Maybe. But I'm the oldest. It's my job to be a dick.

I offer her an expression that isn't murderous, and ask, "What can I get you, Charlotte?"

She considers, her gaze roaming over the stocked bar behind me. "Vodka and soda with a splash of cranberry and a lime."

With a nod, I make her drink, and only then do I deign to look at my brother. What I see almost makes me think he's been abducted by aliens, because the man actually *smiles* at me.

This must be what Darcy meant when she told me how different I appeared when I smiled. Because my brother almost doesn't even look like himself. It's unsettling.

"The usual," he says to my unspoken question.

"Good to know some things haven't changed," I mutter. "Ox?"

He shakes his head and points to the uniform he's wearing. "Not tonight. Figured I'd help deliver the bad news, though."

I pull the top off my brother's favorite beer and slide it towards him, waiting.

Levi grabs it and takes a sip. "Pipes burst at the rec center."

I freeze.

"It's a mess." Ox picks up the story. "No way will they be done in time for the party on Saturday."

"So, we need to move it here," Charlotte finishes, the smile on her face telling me she's heard about my supposed aversion to having it here and is hoping to soften the blow.

All three of them stare at me, and I glare back. "Fine."

"Yes!" Ox pumps a fist. "I knew you'd come around."

"I'll remind you that I offered to have it here," I fire back. "But you said this place wasn't good enough."

"What is your problem?" Levi asks, his characteristic frown back in place as he steps closer.

"Hi!" Darcy appears at the end of the bar, her bright smile

immediately putting an end to the tension. She walks around and nears us, still grinning and holding out a hand. "I'm Darcy. You must be Levi. No mistaking Ox's twin brother."

I bite the inside of my cheek to keep from laughing at Levi's stunned expression. He blinks, once, twice, three times, then seems to pull himself together.

"Um, hi."

Charlotte snorts and moves him out of the way, shaking Darcy's hand as she does. "I'm Charlotte. That immobile hunk of granite is indeed Levi."

Darcy's smile is so fucking bright my heart physically hurts. God *damn*, I love her.

"Darcy is my—" I start, but then I stare at her, lost. What do you call the woman you're totally and thoroughly head over heels for?

"I'm his," she says with a grin. "And he's mine."

Ox squeals. "It's official?" He clutches his chest. "Ugh. *Finally!* I'm so happy right now."

I shake my head, unable to contain the laughter that bubbles up from my throat.

"Holy fuck," Levi breathes. "He just laughed." He looks at his wife, then Ox, then at Darcy before swinging back to me. "Did you—you *laughed.*"

I do it again, then gesture for everyone to have a seat. "Guess it's a night of firsts, then."

"Sit by me," Charlotte commands Darcy. "I already like you, and I need to know way more about you."

Darcy's cheeks go rosy. "I'm in the middle of things with my team, but I'll swing back when I'm through. You're welcome to come hang with us if you don't want to deal with all this." She waves her hands in our direction.

"Done. And you three? Behave." Charlotte pivots on her heel and follows Darcy, leaving the three of us and Aaron staring at each other.

"This should be good," Aaron says, toasting us and leaning back on the stool.

"Lay it on me," I sigh. "What do we need to do?"

Ox brandishes his phone. "I have a list."

CHAPTER 27

DARCY

THE CELEBRATION FOR Anthony's parents is today. And for as wonderful as the rest of our lives currently are, my man has been nothing but stressed about this. The last couple of days he's slept terribly, tossing and turning.

But right now, he's asleep, one inked arm thrown over his head, breaths coming deep and easy from his bare chest, and he's at peace. No trace of the stress that'll immediately fall upon him as soon as he wakes.

Sunlight streams in through the butter-yellow curtains and bathes the room in a warm light. I deliberately picked the color to emphasize the morning sun since the windows face east, and I haven't regretted it once in all the mornings I've woken up here.

Sliding the covers down, I treat myself to the vision that is his impressive, and delightfully naked, form. Hard lines and tight, corded muscles that speak of years of hard work and physical labor, plus the work he's done to hone his body with weights. And speaking of weighty, his morning erection is something to behold. I'm not sure I'll ever get over the way this specimen of a man wants me, but hey, I'm good with it.

I settle between his legs, aware he's woken up because of the way his breathing's changed, but he keeps still, his eyes staying closed, as I lean forward to press my nose against his abdomen. God, he smells so good. Like sleep and fabric softener, along with that signature Anthony scent. It makes me wet. Pressing my legs together, I leave his stomach and turn to his cock, slowly licking up the shaft. The moan that rumbles out of him is low and delicious, his length growing even more in response to my attention.

"Darcy." His voice is soft.

I hum and continue my work, wanting nothing more than to bring this man to orgasm and send him into the day on a high note. His hands thread through my hair, pulling it to the side and giving him a clear view of me. Our eyes meet as I swirl my tongue down and around his erection, and his darken.

"Harder," he commands.

"Woken up feisty, have we?" I smirk.

He tightens his hold on my hair, tugging it in a way that gives me all the pleasure but still lets me know he means what he says. When his next word is, "Please," I merely blink up at him and give him what he wants.

In less than a minute, he's yanking me by my hair up his body. "I need to come inside that tight cunt, Darcy."

"Fuck," I breathe, barely able to balance myself before he's bringing me down onto his cock in one swift, delicious motion. "You're so fucking *big* in the morning."

"Only for you," he grits out, his jaw tense with the effort of holding himself back. He swirls his hips and I moan, following his rhythm like a woman enchanted. "Now ride my cock like a good girl." His fingers dig into my hips.

"I'm close," I gasp.

"Play with your tits, Darcy. Let me see you."

I lever up to squeeze my breasts, the movement adjusting the angle of how he's hitting, and moan at the unfamiliar sensation.

We keep going, our bodies slicking with sweat. His eyes never leave mine.

"I love you," I whisper.

His irises darken to a forest green as he grins naughtily. "Fuck yeah you do."

A surprised laugh bursts out of me, and his entire body flinches at the way it makes my pussy contract around him. "That's what you get," I scold him.

He thrusts into me, and I gasp. "And that's what *you* get, sweet girl. I love you, too. Now do me a favor and come," he urges, moving his hand off my hip so he can press a thumb to my clit and circle it.

The pressure is exactly what I needed, and I throw my head back, losing myself to the heat of his touch. Every part of my body is alive, wild and free, and there, building at the edges of pleasure, is a mounting wave of intensity.

"There it is, yes," he praises. "I can feel you. You're almost there, baby. Squeeze me. I need you to take all my cum."

I whimper, my legs shaking. "It's too—I need—fuck, I—" My words break off, and I give in, shattering.

"There you go—*fuck*." He grunts the last word as I shout and bear down on him, coming so hard that my vision darkens for a moment.

Then he roars, thrusting and holding as he comes, his cock pulsing inside me. I keep rolling my hips, slowly coming to a stop as his chest heaves from the early-morning exertion.

I breathe, sweaty and sated, only slightly beginning to get my bearings. I push my hair away from my face and grin goofily down at him.

He grins right back, then pulls me to his chest, the two of us still connected, and presses a kiss to my forehead. He pulls my hair into his hands, gently working out the tangles as our breathing evens out. After another few minutes, he says, "Good morning."

I giggle. "Good morning."

"Please feel free to wake me up like that any time you want," he says. "Truly. *Any* time."

"Mmm," I hum against his chest. "Only if you fuck me like that when I do."

"Deal."

Chapter 28

Anthony

I'M A BALL of stress. I hate it.

After a shower, Darcy and I head downstairs and see that Harrison's already there, doing his usual morning checks on the machines and cleaning the bowling shoes we rent to the patrons.

"Morning, boss," he chirps, happy as a lark.

I grunt.

Darcy, being the far better human than me, gives him a smile and they make small talk. Harrison's entire demeanor around Darcy changed when he realized I liked her. Smart man.

"I still don't see why we need to close the entire day for this," I grumble.

"Getting people to leave is a lot harder when they're already here." Harrison doesn't miss a beat.

"We could be making money," is all I say in return.

Harrison doesn't bother replying, and Ox, Levi, and Charlotte come through the door next, loaded down with more decorating supplies than I'd prefer to see.

"What do you plan on doing with all of that?" I growl.

"We're decorating, asshole," Levi shoots back at me. "Deal

with it. You don't have to help, but you *do* have to get out of the way."

Charlotte shoots Levi a look, then closes the distance to pull me into a side hug. "Good morning, Grumpy!"

I grumble. It feels nice to default back to the grouch I was before Darcy made me happy.

But all Charlotte does is laugh, and Darcy does the same. With a sidelong glance at my woman, Charlotte observes, "You need more coffee."

"Which is why I brought some." Ox brandishes two carrying containers of iced coffee and hands mine over with a smug smile. He knows exactly how I like it: iced latte with oat milk and three raw sugars. It's the only time I'll indulge in something that tastes like a dessert, and somehow the bastard knew I'd want one.

Darcy accepts the frozen sugary concoction Ox hands her next, moaning almost as loud as when my mouth was on her in the shower upstairs.

I'm still not happy to be having it here, but there really was no other place. The only bright spot is knowing that Levi "this place isn't good enough" Hall hates having it here. Seeing him climbing ladders and cussing when the streamers rip is also pretty damn satisfying.

The hours pass quickly, and soon enough, Reid is at the door, delivering lunch for all of us and promising to come back when he's off duty.

There are more streamers and balloons than I can count, and the place is festooned with photos of my parents as well. Scattered in between are pictures of the five of us, and they hurt to look at. We boys go from scrawny and awkward up to hulking giants, and looking at them just makes me hungry. We were always hungry. Mom struggled to keep us fed, and there were more bologna and rice dinners than I'd prefer.

The background of the trailer park looms in so many of them, too. I never much minded living there, but I know it chapped

Levi's ass in particular. It's why he bought them a house the second he could. Our parents would have stayed in that damn trailer park the rest of their days, despite it being unsafe as hell. The community was never the problem; the actual structure was what put Levi over the edge. And the more that hurricanes and other bad weather increased, the more his urgency became to get them the hell out of there. It was a rare instance of me agreeing wholeheartedly with my brother.

Darcy's hand rests on my back as she approaches, standing next to me to look at one of the pictures. By some miracle, Coach had let us freshman football players have a few days off during the season, so I'd driven the few hours home to catch one of my brothers' games. They were in high school, dressed out in full pads and nearly as tall as me, fresh off a win against some team or another. Mom and Dad bracket us on either side, both of them wearing smiles so proud that even now it almost breaks my heart. Because it was never me they were proud of, despite me playing for the University of Alabama. I remember that distinctly. It was always the twins. That night, my brothers had run some kind of offensive miracle and worked together to score the winning touchdown.

"You weren't happy." Darcy says it so matter-of-factly that I startle, looking at her with my mouth open.

She laughs. "Don't look so surprised. I know your expressions. I know when your smile is actually a shield, and I know that most of your scowls are actually forms of a smile."

Her words are a balm, and I feel myself defrost the tiniest bit. "Thank you."

She tilts her head up for a kiss, then studies me. "Was it really so bad? Growing up with them?"

I open my mouth to speak, but don't have the words. Yes, it was. No, it wasn't. It's so fucking complicated.

She gives an understanding chuckle and hugs me. "Come on. I think the guests are arriving."

It's a relief to lose myself to bartending for a while, and I half want to stay there when Harrison shows up an hour later to tell me my parents are there. "Go mingle and shit," he says with a smirk. "I know how much you love that."

I give a derisive snort as I toss the towel on the bar. "Watch out or I'll fire you."

He laughs. "You couldn't handle this place without me."

Mom and Dad are surrounded by people, and it takes them a long time to finally reach my brothers and me.

"There are my boys!" Dad opens his arms and gestures for Ox and Levi, the same way he always does. I swear I'm an afterthought.

But Mom turns to me for a hug, and it's surprising to get her attention first. "Hi, Mom."

She pats my back, then steps back and takes my arms in her hands, giving me a once-over. "How are you, my firstborn?"

"Fine, Mom. Thanks."

Dad finally releases the twins and shoots me a cheerful grin. "Anthony!" But he doesn't step forward for a hug. Just nods and smiles.

It hurts more than it should.

Charlotte and Darcy appear on the periphery, and after Charlotte says her hellos, Mom looks expectantly at all of us to figure out who the extra woman in our circle is.

"This is Darcy," is all I say.

Hurt flashes across Darcy's face, but she covers it as she holds out a hand to shake theirs. "I never took your classes, Mr. Hall, but I remember you well."

Dad chuckles. "Ah, one of the lucky ones, huh?"

She smiles, and I can see just how fake it is. "Something like that." When her gaze darts to mine, clearly wondering why the hell I'm not saying what she means to me to them, all I can do is grind my teeth. They don't deserve her sunshine.

Makes no damn sense, but I just…don't want to share her with them. I don't want to share my happiness with them.

Jesus, I sound like an ass when I say that. Is that really what I think? I don't know.

I excuse myself, but no one really seems to notice. And *that's* the reason, right there. I could probably run around in a purple gorilla suit and they'd not notice, as wrapped up as they are in each other.

Darcy makes herself scarce, too, and I deserve nothing less. When Ox finds me to bring out the cake—because I'm the one who knows where it is, not because I should be included in the celebrations—I do my best to put on a show. It's not about me, I know that. My parents are happy. Healthy. Living in a house that Levi bought them. They're loved by so many people in our community.

The cake is delicious, made by yet another local former student of Dad's, but it turns to ash in my mouth as Ox asks Reid to take a picture of just him and Levi with Mom and Dad.

"Anthony! Get in here!" Mom calls.

I ignore her, turning to leave.

"Anthony," comes another call, only this time it's in the unmistakable growl of Levi. The fuck if I care. He calls my name again, and I keep walking.

"What in the fuck is your problem?" His hand flicks the back of my arm as I charge around the corner, away from the prying eyes of the partygoers.

"Nothing."

"Bullshit," he shoots back. "Look at me and tell me what's got you so worked up."

"It doesn't matter," I say, steeling my voice. And it really doesn't. I could tell them all, explain that I was tired of always being an afterthought, even though I was the first fucking born. That for just one day, I'd enjoy being someone that they were all proud of instead of being the one they squinted their eyes about and pretended to be excited that I'd opened a gaming hall.

"You need to go back out there and apologize to Mom."

I bark out a laugh. "Absolutely not."

Levi steps closer. "That woman sacrificed everything for us—"

"Yeah, yeah. Blah blah, I know, Levi. I *know*. I was there. I was there the whole fucking time—not that any of you seem to remember that little fact."

"Oh, what kind of bullshit are you talking about?" Levi drawls, his eyes flashing. "Don't tell me you're *jealous*."

"Of you?" I scoff. "Hardly."

He steps into my space, sneering. "Then get the fuck back out there and tell our mother that you're sorry."

"Fuck off," I seethe. And I know I shouldn't, but this asshole has pushed me too fucking far. I use my height to my advantage, jerking my shoulders back and pushing my chest out to force him back.

It's enough to make him snap, and he's cocking his fist back and sending it swinging towards me before I can process he's truly done it.

His fist slams into my cheek, and pain—beautiful, easily identifiable pain—blooms as my head jerks back.

I see red.

Immediately, I throw my own punch. It lands exactly where I want it, on his upper cheek and grazing his eye. Fucker still doesn't know how to protect himself in a fight.

He lunges, and I let him tackle me, needing the physicality of it like I need to fucking breathe.

We're tangled up, landing blow after blow on each other's ribs and anywhere else we can, when Ox and Reid's unmistakable voices yell at us to break it up.

Reid pulls me back and Ox takes Levi, both of them in full cop mode based on the brutal grip Reid has on me. My arms are pinned behind my back, and I legitimately have no idea how he's incapacitated me.

"Let me go," I growl.

"Not a fucking chance," he grunts, clearly having to work to keep his grip on me.

"What the fuck, guys?" Ox demands, his own grip on Levi just as secure.

"Let me go," Levi says, his voice low and deadly. "I'll give him one more punch and we'll be good."

I jerk at Reid's grip and snarl a laugh. "That's the only way you'll make it happen, asshole. You need me held back because you can't fucking do it yourself. Like *always*."

The words hit home, and he leaps to get closer, Ox shouting and holding him tighter.

"You need to get out of here," Reid says in my ear. "Go upstairs and stay there. Do not come back."

Because he assumes it's my fault. This is my fucking place, and yet I'm the one being told to leave. Which tracks. Of course it tracks. Reid doesn't know shit about our family dynamics and even *he* sides with the twins. Every. Fucking. Time.

I twist out of his grip and lift a hand to my swelling cheek, feeling the spot just above my beard where he broke the skin. Without a word to anyone, I walk away.

CHAPTER 29

DARCY

I LOSE COUNT of the number of people who ask where Anthony's gone. All I can do is shrug and make up a story about him not feeling well. Which I know is a lie, because I saw everything.

He didn't see me as he strode past the bar and yanked open the door that leads upstairs to his loft. He didn't seem to see much of anything. When I turned to follow him, Charlotte was there, putting her hand on my arm and shaking her head, telling me to give him some time to himself.

Now that the party is over and I'm helping clean up, and his parents keep shooting questioning glances over at me as though they're trying to decide if I'm someone important to this situation or not, I deeply regret listening to her. But I don't want Anthony to walk down tomorrow morning and have to clean up a party he clearly wasn't in the mood to have, and I'm the only one who knows where anything is. Harrison dipped out hours ago, and I wasn't about to try making the part-time kids from the high school stay for the clean-up.

Which means I'm desperately wishing I'd followed Anthony the way I wanted to. Every time I pass Levi, his face seems to get more mottled with a massive bruise, and the rueful smile he shoots me as we clear the tables in the party room doesn't really communicate that he's sorry. When the last balloon is popped and the trash is in the dumpster outside, I make myself scarce with a last nod at Ox, who offers his trademark broad smile in return.

Is Ox not worried about the situation? Or maybe he is, but he knows that both his brothers need a cooling-off period. It makes me realize just how little I know about their family. I'd always figured the brothers were all close, but after seeing the rage and hurt on Anthony's face as he walked away, I know I was very, very wrong.

"Anthony?" I sweep my gaze around the loft, expecting to find him shooting pool or even lifting weights in the tiny area against a far wall. I double-check my phone but no missed calls or texts from him, either. "Anthony? You here?"

Silence.

Then it hits me. I know exactly where he is.

I see him the second I reach the apex of the dunes, sitting on the sand and angled to watch the sun dip into the horizon. I watch him for a good five minutes, but he stays in position, his knees drawn up and his arms wrapped around them, brooding like the top-tier grump he likes everyone to think he is.

I know better these days. I know the shield he puts up is for everyone else. All the same, he's got some explaining to do, because the asshole made a deliberate choice when he introduced me to his parents. He's not hesitated to let the world know about our relationship, but the second his parents are *right there*, he goes mute. Then he gets in a fight with his brother?

He turns his head as I approach, then returns his gaze to the ocean.

And that's it. I may love him, but I am *done* with being the quiet, understanding girlfriend. I gave it a solid three hours, and I've gotta say, it sucks. Not my vibe in the least.

So. We're done with that approach.

Instead, I stomp forward, unscrewing the top of my very full, extra giant ice water, and pull the lid into my left hand. He doesn't pay me any mind as I near, which is good, because it allows me to get right up on him before dumping the ice water all over his head.

He jumps up with a roar, his eyes flashing as rivulets of water drip down his face. "What the fuck was that for?"

As calmly as you please, I screw the cup's lid back on. "*You* are being an asshole, and you needed to cool off. I helped."

His eyes narrow, and it emphasizes the mottled skin around his left eye that is, somewhat impressively, almost a dead match for the one his brother has. When he speaks, it's laced with a dismissive cruelty I've not heard before. "Go away, Darcy. Leave me alone and go home."

My spine straightens as he tries to turn away. But he's got another thing coming if he thinks I'm letting him act like this. "You owe me an apology," I say, reaching to touch his arm and bring his attention back to me. "*And* you need to get your shit together and stop acting like a child!"

He scoffs. "That's rich coming from you."

"And what does that mean?"

He throws his arms wide, water droplets flinging. "That you're the child here!"

Did he *really* just go there? "Oh, fuck you, Anthony."

He shifts on his feet, crossing his arms and smirking. And for the first time, he doesn't look sexy or hot at all. He looks cold. Heartless. "Tell me I'm wrong."

Hackles up, I shout back, "You're wrong!"

"No," he says, his voice so low I almost don't hear it over the ocean. "I'm not. You're twenty-four, Darcy. Twenty. Four. I, on the other hand, am a forty-one-year-old man who's got no business with someone like you. You. Are. A. Child."

Anger flares hot and bright and I blink furiously, praying the tears don't come. I take a step back, refusing to let him see how his words hurt. "You are so fucking bitter," I spit. "And for what? Your parents didn't pay enough attention to you? Grow the fuck up. At least you *had* a mother, Anthony. Sure, you were the oldest to twins and had to figure stuff out a lot faster than you would have otherwise. You poor baby. You know what I had? A single father who didn't know what to do with me for years, but he fucking tried, and there were times he absolutely messed up, but he loved me. Could things be better? Sure. Is he perfect? Definitely not. But we *talk*. When was the last fucking time you pulled your head out of your ass and actually *talked* to your parents? Did you ever think that this is a two-way street? Huh?"

He blinks, as though none of this has actually occurred to him. "There's more to it than that," he finally says quietly.

"I'm sure there is," I sigh. "But you haven't told me *anything* about this, Anthony. Nothing. You and I are a two-way street, as well."

His jaw ticks, but he says nothing else.

I laugh. It's all I can do, because I don't have any more water to dump on him. Clueless fucking man. "And you think *I'm* the child?" I take another step back, then another, shaking my head the whole time. "I love you, I do. You have some serious work to do on yourself. Call me when you come to your senses and you're ready to apologize."

Men. *Ugh*.

Chapter 30

Anthony

I WATCH HER leave, my thoughts scrambling, my throat working to swallow the baseball-sized lump in it, and all I can think is, *damn*. Damn that woman. That infuriating, beautiful—one hundred percent *correct*—woman. This whole time I thought I was teaching her, when really, she was the one teaching me.

Again: dammit.

"Your parents didn't pay enough attention to you? Grow the fuck up. At least you had a mother, Anthony. Sure, you were the oldest to twins and had to figure stuff out a lot faster than you would have otherwise. You poor baby."

Her words swirl around my head, and wow, I sound like a shithead.

Have I really been like this the whole time?

All my actions with my brothers, the past two decades in particular, and the way I've been with my parents. Has it all been my fault?

Fuck it all to hell.

Crouching down and shoving my hand through my hair, I yell at the sand. Then I leap up and yell at the ocean. This is all my fault. I've never bothered to say anything to my parents or my brothers, and here I am, literally yelling at the world because I have absolutely fucked up.

I take a few minutes to consider my next move. I could go after Darcy, tell her I was wrong, and she was completely, without question, right about everything she said, and beg her to forgive me. The thing is, I'm not sure she'd believe me. Darcy's a woman who believes in action. And I've got a lot to *do*, starting with my family.

With my mind made up, I head to my parents' house. The drive is only about twenty minutes down the road that abuts the shoreline, which doesn't give me a lot of time to think. And that's probably for the best, because I don't need to think. I need to feel. And *then* I can think about how I feel.

I snort. I have no idea if that makes any sense. Guess I need to be okay with that, though, because for once, I don't care if any of this makes me sound like some kind of woo-woo person. Not when ignoring my feelings has gotten me here, where I'm forty-one and the woman I love is telling me in no uncertain terms to grow up. The woman who is seventeen years younger than me, for fuck's sake.

Dad opens the door with a raised brow. "Since when do you knock?"

"Since I behaved like an ass." Might as well dive in headfirst.

With a chuckle, Dad steps back to let me in. "Son, that's your default setting." He slaps my back as I walk in. "Not sure I'd recognize you any other way."

Well, if that's not illuminating, I don't know what is.

Stopping in the hallway, I turn to him. "Why didn't you hug me earlier tonight?"

He considers me for all of two seconds. "Because you told us you didn't like hugs when you were a kid. And we wanted to respect that."

Shaken, I ask, "I...what? When did I say that?"

"It's been a long time, so I can't quite recall. Maybe when you were eight or nine?"

"You were ten." Mom comes up behind Dad and wraps a slender arm around his waist. "And you declared that not only were you no longer accepting hugs, but that you didn't want to be used as the twins' personal jungle gym, either." Her smile is affectionate. "It was nearly impossible to keep the boys off you, but your father and I figured respecting your boundaries ourselves was the least we could do."

The memory niggles at the back of my mind, just out of reach.

"Is this about earlier?" Mom asks gently.

Shame flames my cheeks as I hang my head. "It is. I came to apologize."

"Well, come on in, then. May as well do it with an audience," Dad says, winking at me. Then he lowers his voice and smiles at me. "And if you want a hug, I'd love to give you one."

My throat tightens. "I would."

He opens his arms wide, and I step into them. His hug is strong, and it feels like home. We stand there, both of us gripping the other tight, for longer than is probably necessary. But it feels good, and I think if anyone deserves a too-long hug, it's my dad. And my mom.

Releasing him, I turn to Mom, who's got her own arms open. This time, it's she who steps into my embrace, and I wonder when she got so small. "I love you, Mom."

"Love you, too, firstborn," she murmurs against my chest. Pulling back, she looks up at me. "You ready?"

I grit my teeth. "As I'll ever be."

Everyone's here. Not just Ox, but Levi and Charlotte, all of whom look up in surprise to see me standing here.

"The fuck are you doing here?" Levi growls, an ice pack held against his eye.

"To say I'm sorry." It's more than a little gratifying to see the look of surprise on his face. The bruises are pretty great, too. Turning to my parents, I ask, "May I sit?"

Mom leads me to the smaller couch, and we sit side by side. "Tell us what's on your mind, little one."

I can't help but laugh. "And here I was, wondering when you got so small."

She places a hand on my biceps and leans into me, smiling. "When you got to high school."

It's a reminder of why I'm here. I take a deep breath. "I have some apologies to make."

Ox grins knowingly at me. "Did Darcy give you hell?"

My neck heats. "Maybe."

Charlotte laughs softly, and she looks at Levi with satisfaction. "Amazing what a good woman can do, isn't that right, Levi?"

He doesn't respond, merely palms the inside of her thigh and pulls her closer, the look of adoration on his face making him seem like a totally different person.

"Darcy?" Dad prompts. "As in Darcy Belle, the girl we briefly met tonight?"

"Of course, Darcy Belle," Mom chides him. "Wasn't it obvious?"

"Was what obvious?" Dad asks.

"That they're dating," Mom answers, then looks at me. "Right?"

"Yes," I confirm. "But it's not just dating. It's..." I trail off, my instinct to keep it to myself rearing its head. But no. That's what got me here. "It's more than that. I love her. A lot. She's it for me." If she'll still have me, that is. But I keep that part to myself.

"Why didn't you say something?" Mom prods.

"Because I'm an ass." I shift to look at her, but make sure that Dad knows I'm speaking to him, too. "And Darcy made sure I knew it."

"You've been an ass your whole life," Levi grumbles.

"I know that now."

"*Now?* You just *now* know it?" Ox's jaw drops, and even though his tone is teasing, there's real hurt in his eyes.

"I just now realize how much of it was hurtful," I clarify. "And I'm going to work on it," I promise, then gesture at Levi's eye. "But you deserved that."

He lifts a shoulder and offers a small smile. "It's fine. Besides, it's good to see I gave just as good as I got."

The joke breaks the tension, and I give my attention back to Mom and Dad. "Darcy made sure I understood that I've got some things to work through, but I'll start by saying how sorry I am for the way I've acted."

Mom pats my leg and Dad nods. "Good," he answers. "Because you've hurt your mother's heart more times than I can count."

The directness of his words hit home, and my throat tightens. Looking directly into her eyes, I apologize. "I'm sorry, Mom. I've been a self-centered prick—"

"Your entire life," she interjects. "Not just since the twins came home."

My lips twitch up. "Really?"

She nods, but then says, "No, not really—but it was fun to see how seriously you took it just now."

"Oh-ho, Mom's got jokes!" Ox laughs.

"*But* we have our own apologies to make," she continues, reaching for my hand and squeezing it. "We're your parents. There are a lot of things we could have done, could have *said*, to do better by you."

"Like telling you how proud we were of you for all your accomplishments," Dad says, drawing my attention to him. "Coming to more of your college games."

"Those were expensive," I interject.

"We could have saved up," Mom replies. "And we should have reached out more once you came home."

Dad nods. "I'm sorry, son. It was unforgiveable."

My throat tightens. What was it that Darcy said? *Did you ever think that maybe it's a two-way street?* She was right. Again. "It's not unforgiveable," I manage to say past the lump in my throat. "We all played a part."

Mom grins mischievously. "You really did complain a lot. Your brothers never did, but you?"

We all guffaw. "Mom," Levi wheezes, "we *all* complained."

"The summers with no electricity?" Ox reminds her.

Mom waves us away. "That was *one* summer—"

"Two," I correct.

"Fine. Two summers, but it was only a week at a time, and we just made it an adventure," she huffs.

"We were in middle school," Levi says. "There was nothing *adventurous* about it."

"I don't know," Ox muses. "I think it gave us character."

I snort. "It gave us something, all right." But for once, as I think back over those early hard years, the ones where we were likely a lot poorer than my brothers and I realized, there's no bitterness. Running my own place now, I understand how difficult it can be to simply make enough to pay the bills. Thankfully, I'm well past that stage, but there were some months when I first opened Hall's Balls that I really wasn't sure I'd make it. Ironically, it was Levi who offered to help float me if I needed it, and the man definitely had the cash to spare. I didn't take it. In hindsight, my ego was so delicate that I probably would have closed the place before I took help from my little brother. I'm glad it never came to that.

"I should apologize, too," Levi says, his voice so low that I barely hear him.

My eyes snap to his.

The faintest red tinges his cheeks. "I was probably more of an asshole than I needed to be."

Ox snorts. "*Was?*"

Levi glowers at him before looking back at me. "Fine. I *am* more of an asshole than I need to be."

I shrug and grin. "It's cool. You've learned from the best."

"Maybe we'll have a contest to see who's got the meanest-looking scowl," Ox teases. "It'll be close."

"Shut up, Ox," Levi and I say in unison.

Mom wraps an arm around me and squeezes. "We love you, little one."

Dad nods and holds my gaze. "Proud of you, too."

He'd said something similar a moment ago, but this time, the words unlock something in my chest, and I blink back the sting in my eyes.

"Was really something to see your place today," he continues, not seeming to realize how much his words have affected me. "We should have visited a lot more than we have. You've done a great job with it."

"You really have. But that name, Anthony," Mom says with an air of resigned exasperation. "Hall's *Balls*? It's so…crude."

My brothers and I laugh. And it feels amazing.

Chapter 31

Darcy

SUNDAY MORNING YOGA isn't the same without Anthony. I didn't exactly expect to see him here, but I did hope. I worried about him all last night and literally had to turn my phone off and put it under the couch to keep me from checking it constantly.

And when I woke up this morning and dug it out, it honestly sucked to see he hadn't reached out. But I *did* tell him to reach out once he had his shit together, so…I guess I need to be patient.

Amanda casts a worried look at me as the instructor calls the class to order. "You okay?"

I nod stiffly. Because I have to be okay. I have to trust that Anthony will do the very thing I told him he needed to do. And I have to wait.

I can't focus. Every pose feels forced, and Amanda keeps looking at me like I might burst into tears at any moment. Probably because I keep huffing and puffing, thanks to my inability to get focused. It's all shit. I'm jittery and it feels like I have ants in my pants.

Halfway through, I give up, nodding an apology at Amanda

and the instructor as I roll my mat and pick my way to the door. I burst outside and practically run to the edge of the boardwalk, bending over and taking deep breaths.

"Darcy? You okay?" Ox's voice breaks through my jumbled thoughts.

With a final exhale, I look up, shielding my eyes from the sun as I find myself in front of Anthony's little brother. "Hi, Chief."

He huffs a smile. "Please. You're practically family. I'm Ox."

I shift on my feet. "I don't know if that's true," I admit. "But thanks."

"Oh, it's true." He smiles. "Don't worry."

I give him a rueful grin. "If you say so."

"I do," he says cheerily. "Whatever you said to him last night worked, because he came to Mom and Dad's last night and apologized." He steps forward and lowers his voice into a conspiratorial whisper. "I don't know if you know this, but Anthony doesn't apologize."

My chest warms at his words. "Yeah?"

"Yeah."

"Well, good," I say.

Ox studies me. "He hasn't been in touch yet, has he?" At my answering shake of my head, he continues, "Give him time. I don't know what went down between the two of you, but he's definitely doing what you told him to do. That much I can guarantee."

I want to believe him. "Thanks, Ox."

He smiles. "Any time, Darcy." The radio on his shoulder goes off, the words a mumble that I can't quite make out. He cocks his head to it, listening, then presses a button. "Chief here. I'm close by. I'll check it out." Then he looks back at me. "I'll see you soon?"

"Hope so," I offer.

He winks. "I know so."

I watch him walk away, the anxiety coursing through my body having calmed a bit at Ox's words. But I'm still uneasy.

My phone dings, and I check the screen. It's Dad, needing my help at the store. I blow out a breath and send him a note that I'll be there shortly.

I find him where he almost always is: at the front, greeting customers like he's known them his whole life. Which he has. Dad grew up not far from here, fell in love with his high school sweetheart, and stayed here. When she died, I was a baby. I don't have any memories of her; just photos of her holding me in her arms with a contented smile.

"Darcy!" He looks up and smiles, his eyes lighting up as he sees me. "Thanks for coming."

I lean in for a hug. "Of course. What's going on?"

He hesitates. "I know you said you don't want to work here full-time," he begins.

I stiffen. "Dad," I warn. "You better not be trying to talk me out of this."

"I'm not, I promise." He holds his hands up in surrender. "I have a request, though." A beat. "Two, actually."

Crossing my arms defensively, I ask, "And they are?"

He grins. "First, I need you to show me how the damn accounting software works."

"Only if you promise to actually pay attention this time."

"Pinkie promise." He holds his out.

Hooking my pinkie to his, I meet his eyes. "That's serious."

"I know."

We tighten the grip, then move our hands up and down in a shake. "Deal. And the second thing?"

"Call JJ and see about putting an ad in the paper."

"For what?"

He unhooks his pinkie. "You're fired."

"What?" I choke out. I didn't hear him correctly.

His smile is kind. "Sweet girl, I'm pretty sure you won't *really* stop working here if I don't make you. And I'll keep finding ways to hang onto you. So, this is me trying, the only way I know how."

I sniff. "Seriously?"

He holds his arms out for an embrace, and I step into them. The hug he gives me is warm and tight, and it releases something deep inside me. I exhale and hug him back.

"You forgive me?" he asks.

"For firing me? I'm not sure how I feel about it yet."

He laughs, the sound muffled by my ear being pressed against his chest. "Something tells me you'll get over it. But I meant about Anthony."

We release each other and I look up at him. "Anthony?"

He nods, a serious expression taking over his face. "I wasn't very understanding when I first found out."

"Which is why I called you out on it immediately," I point out.

He grimaces. "Oh, I remember."

"And your timing was shit," I continue. "I'd just gotten fourth place in a tournament and was so happy, and you're all *can we talk* and *what the hell is this*," I mimic him, lowering my voice even as I grin.

"I know, I know," he says. "I just want you to know that no matter what, I've got your back, Darcy girl. And I'm sorry I didn't behave that way at first. It's...well, it just took me by surprise, that's all."

"I accept your apology. Now, are you paying me severance?" I ask cheekily.

Dad makes a huffing sound. "Get outta here with that mess."

Chapter 32

Anthony

PATIENCE, IT TURNS out, is not a quality I possess. Because I spend a solid hour staring at the ceiling as the sun rises, trying like hell to decide what to do. Do I call her? Show up at her door and beg for her forgiveness?

I check the time. Six a.m. I fling the covers off and throw on shorts and running shoes, then gulp down a glass of water and head out for a run on the beach. I need to clear my head. There's still so much for me to work through, but hell if I'm going to do that without Darcy by my side. If she'll still have me, that is.

Water laps up the shoreline as I run, seagulls swooping and diving fifty yards out in the ocean as I try to remember the last time I felt so hopeful. Yes, I have mounds of issues that I clearly need to work through, but for the first time, I can take a solid breath without it feeling like my chest is going to crack.

With a smile, I bear down and run faster.

I fully intended to head straight to Darcy's after a shower, but Harrison is already downstairs and intercepts me before I can make my escape.

"We're booked solid today," he calls over his shoulder. Then he turns and yelps, feigning shock. "What...what is that on your face?"

I reach up but find nothing out of place.

"Your lips. They're...smiling?" He pauses. "Are you ill? Feverish? Did that punch Levi landed knock a few screws loose?"

"Fuck off," I chuckle good-naturedly.

"Well, I'm glad you're in a good mood, because it's all hands on deck today."

"I need to—" I start.

"Help me like the owner you are?" Harrison finishes. "Excellent!"

I sigh. "Is it that bad? I really need—"

"Boss."

"Harrison."

"When's the last time I actually asked you for help?"

I consider. "Never?"

He snaps and points a finger at me. "Bingo."

In no time at all, we'd stocked everything up for the day and opened, then were swarmed with one party after another. We ran ragged, and while normally I'd have taken up my station behind the bar, there was no time to do anything but serve a few beers and run right back onto the floor. Which meant that I got to be on the receiving end of a slightly panicked father who was running point on a birthday party for his four-year-old.

The dude clearly needed some help, but at the same time, it was comforting to see how all the other dads came together to wrangle the little wild things for the party. I comped a pitcher of beer for them, and you'd have thought I was Santa Claus with the grateful looks they gave me.

"Our wives thought it'd be a great idea for us to run one of these ourselves," the host dad said, clutching his plastic cup of beer like it was a lifeline. "And I thought, how hard can it be? Me and the guys figured this was the safest place to do it. They're contained, they've got game tokens, easy."

I stared at him and waited for the punchline. There was nothing easy about little kids' birthday parties. Not unless you were an oblivious asshole who let your kids run rampant with no regard for anyone else. I may not have kids, but run a place that's regularly filled to the brim with them, and you learn some things real fast.

"Anyway," he said with a squirm, "thanks for the beer."

I grunted and walked away, no longer comforted in the least.

Surprising no one, I was back in that same party room an hour later, cleaning up puke from where none of the dads paid attention to the little girl who ate not one, but *five* cupcakes fast as lightning. It would be funny if it weren't gross.

Half an hour later, I finally finish cleaning up the mess and scrub my hands for all I'm worth, then find Harrison at the front helping the same little girl pick a prize for the insane number of tickets she's somehow cobbled together. With her prize picked, she skips off with a smile.

I meet Harrison's eyes. "That girl is going to be a handful."

He laughs. "And good for her."

"Good point," I acknowledge. "And when she grows up, she'll be a woman who knows what she wants."

Reid and Matty saunter in, Midnight and Killer strapped to each of their chests. I raise an eyebrow. "No animals, guys. No matter how adorable they are."

Matty grins. "We wanted to check on you."

"Nice bruise," Reid says, lifting his chin at the faint blue surrounding the wound on my cheek.

I exhale. "Yeah. I deserved it."

"Did you *also* deserve the verbal ass-kicking that Darcy gave you? Because I bet it was epic." Reid's eyes are lit up with the possibility of fresh gossip.

Harrison rubs his hands from behind the counter. "Ooh, what's all this? I wasn't going to ask about the face, but clearly, I left too early yesterday."

I point my finger at Reid. "I'm not telling you shit," I proclaim. To Harrison, I say, "And you're getting a raise and title change. Now go do something worthy of it."

His eyes widen. "Really?"

"Yes, really," I say gruffly. "Beat it before I change my mind."

He practically leaves a dust trail.

Turning back to the guys, I motion them outside and follow. Squinting up at the bright blue sky, I take a deep breath and let it out. "Let me guess: Ox told you two?"

"Who else?" Matty answers. "By the way, how do you feel about cats?"

"Don't answer that," Reid interjects. "Unless you want a litter roaming around your loft."

"I'm allergic," I deadpan. The fact that I'm scratching Midnight under her chin notwithstanding.

Matty narrows his eyes. "I think you're lying."

I grin. "Guess you'll never know."

"I think Darcy needs a kitten, don't you?"

Reid pretends to think. "I bet that Agatha does, even if Darcy doesn't."

Matty's eyes light up. "Excellent call." He starts to leave, waving as he goes. "See you later, man."

Reid points two fingers at his eyes and then back to me in a classic *I'm watching you* move as he starts to back away. "Don't fuck this up, man."

I raise my hands. "Working on it."

"You better be. She's perfect for you."

I huff a laugh. "Believe me, I'm well aware."

The rest of the day is interminable. But we finally close, and I head upstairs for a shower. I've got a woman to apologize to.

I find her exactly where I figured I would, back in Agatha's garage that has steadily morphed into a full-on workshop over the months I've seen it. Gone are the lawn care tools and potting soil, replaced by tools I can't name, and stacks of wood propped off the ground. Noah Kahan blares as usual from a speaker on the workbench, and Darcy bends over the lathe, her back to me, clad in her sexy-as-hell overalls. Sawdust flies as she holds what looks to be a table leg in place, the sound of the lathe barely drowned out by the music. I can picture her face, the concentration in her ice-blue eyes behind the plastic safety glasses, the way her bottom lip is sucked into her mouth, held in place by her teeth but slowly being released as she finishes with the task at hand.

I love her.

I love her so damn much.

She straightens, finishing the area and turning the lathe off, the act of which makes the music seem that much louder. With an exhale, she pulls the safety glasses off and sets them to the side, then releases the leg from the lathe and holds it up to inspect it. I can't see if she's pleased with the work or not.

"It's beautiful," I say.

She startles and jerks her head my way, her widened eyes relaxing when she realizes it's me. "Anthony."

I offer a smile. "Hi."

She steps around to the speaker and lowers the volume, and when she turns back to me, her cheeks are flushed. "I wasn't sure you'd want to speak to me again after what I said yesterday."

I gape at her. "Seriously? Woman, *I'm* the one who should say that. After I behaved the way I did—said the things I said—shit, Darcy. I'm so sorry."

Her lips, free of her usual red lipstick but no less devastating, tilt up. "Ox was right."

Furrowing my brow, I ask, "What do you mean?"

She shrugs. "I saw him this morning after I ran out of yoga, and he basically told me you'd come to your senses."

I straighten from where I've been leaning against the side of the garage. "He's correct. Amazing what having a literal bucket of ice water dumped on a man will do to his perspective."

"It wasn't a bucket," she protests with a laugh, her eyes bright and playful.

"Sure felt like it." I move toward her. "And it was cold as fuck."

"I'm not apologizing for it." She juts her chin up.

"Nor would I ever dare ask you to," I murmur, wrapping my hand around her waist and pulling her to me.

She doesn't relent, keeping her body stiff in my grasp. "You should know I won't hesitate to do it again, either."

I huff a laugh. "I would expect nothing less." Tilting my head down to hers, I bring our mouths close. "I'm sorry. Truly. I'm going to do better."

"Good."

"I love you."

She smirks. "I know."

I swat her ass. "Brat."

Her smile widens as she wraps her arms around my neck. "I love you, too."

With a laugh, I slant my mouth over hers, capturing her lips in a kiss that has never felt sweeter.

Epilogue: One Year Later

Darcy

"And the trophy goes to Hall's Belles!"

The four of us squeal and grip each other tight, then I step forward to take the trophy and hoist it above my head. "We won!"

Amanda, Devon, and Agatha surround me, and we cheer once more, jumping up and down and generally losing our minds. It's probably a little over the top, but I don't care.

"Smile!" Aaron calls from somewhere to our right.

We all turn, each of us holding the trophy, and grin like maniacs. Winning the Mobile Regional Bowling Tournament isn't going to put us on the road to professional bowling or anything, but we practiced so hard this past year. Even got another couple of teams up and running at Hall's Balls, so who knows? Maybe we'll start our own baby tournament.

We break apart, each of us heading to our respective people. Devon is swept into Aaron's arms, while Agatha's daughter Betty coos over her and hands her a thermos of iced tea. My dad stands off to the side, his proud gaze bouncing between me and Betty. She and Dad finally stopped hiding their budding romance, and they couldn't be cuter. Then there's Amanda stepping into Harrison's arms—because *that* happened, talk about a plot twist!—and my grouchy hot bartender glowers at me from where he stands a little farther away.

I lick my lips as I close the distance, not missing the way his eyes dart down to watch before raising back up.

"Your approach on that last frame was sloppy," he admonishes.

I bite back a smile. "Was it, now?"

He nods, deadly serious. "It was a miracle you got that spare."

I wrap my arms around his waist and tuck myself against him, making sure he's got a good view of my tits. "Sure was," I agree. Then I sigh dramatically. "If only our coach would just, I don't know, coach us or something."

A corner of his mouth quirks. "You little brat."

I wink. "You gonna spank me later?"

He pretends to consider it. "Only if you're good."

"And if I'm bad?" I counter.

He brings his lips to my ear and speaks low. "Then I'll make you swallow my cock."

I shiver with delight.

"You two done over there?" Harrison calls, breaking up our party of two.

I turn and Anthony's hand wraps around my waist before dipping to squeeze my ass. "For now," Anthony hedges.

We walk outside, with Agatha carrying the trophy like it's her baby.

"Party back at Hall's?" Amanda asks.

"Of course," Harrison answers, pulling her to him for a quick kiss.

"We're celebrating more than our win," I say. "I accepted my fiftieth order today!"

My friends shout and whoop, and the smile on my face is probably big enough to crack me in two. This past year has been a wild ride. A celebrity bought one of my pool tables and posted about it on social media, and business exploded. I ended up renting a workshop a block off the main road in our downtown and have been so busy that I've had to turn down more orders than I've accepted. I'm interviewing apprentices, of all things.

Anthony asked me to move in with him a few months ago, and I agreed. My little cottage was barely getting slept in as it was, so we made it official. No one's moved in yet, but we all figure it's just a matter of time before someone does. And who knows? Maybe that guy Chad will finally get a girlfriend out of it.

We're greeted by a chorus of cheers when we get to Hall's Balls. Reid and Willa are there, along with Matty and Goldie. Ox and Anthony's parents are there, too. Even Levi and Charlotte are in the crowd, along with what looks like half the town.

"What's all this?" I ask Anthony.

"You four are hometown champions," he says. "We needed to be sure you were properly celebrated."

I shake my head, grinning. "You're ridiculous."

He pulls me into a hug. "Maybe. But I love you."

I look up at him and wonder how it is that I've gotten so lucky. Then again, he's gotten lucky, too.

Much later, after I get that promised spanking and give Anthony head with my eyes covered by my bandana, we're curled into each other on the bed. The windows are open to let in the unseasonably cool weather, and the sound of ocean waves drift through the curtains.

"Marry me."

I blink, then blink again. "Did you—"

"Marry me, Darcy," he says again, turning on his side and resting his head in his hand.

I can barely see him in the dark of the room. "Anthony Hall. You can't ask me to marry you in the middle of the night."

His fingers caress my skin, roaming down my arm and around a breast, then up my chest and neck before finding my chin and tipping it up to meet his mouth in a kiss. "But I just did," he counters.

I huff out an adoring laugh. "Ask me in the morning."

And don't you know, that's exactly what he does. When I come to, I find the man looking at me, his hair mussed from sleep, still lying on his side with his head in his hand. Only now, in the daylight, he's holding a gold and ruby filigreed ring up for my inspection.

"Good morning," he grins. "Marry me."

I say yes.

ALSO BY VALERIE PEPPER

GUIDED TO LOVE

~Small town romcom with men in uniform~

The Mechanic's Guide to Getting the Boss's Daughter (series prequel novella)

The Widow's Guide to Second Chances (Book 1)

The Barista's Guide to The Perfect Steam (Book 2)

The Grump's Guide to Chaos (Book 3)

LUCKY IN LOVE

~Beach town romcom shenanigans~

Dining for Love (Book 1)

Dashing for Love (Book 2)

Late to Love (Book 3)

SACRED RIVER

~Small town…with witches!~

Love Potion No. 69 (Novella, Book 1)

Karaoke Chemistry (Book 2)

STANDALONE NOVELS

Lightning in A Bottle (Angsty rockstar road trip romance)

STANDALONE NOVELLAS

Naughty All The Way (November 2023)

To Have and To Scold in the *Holidays & Hook-Ups* anthology by The New Romance Cafe (June 2023 - limited edition)

Acknowledgments

Thank you, as always, to my family for their unwavering support and love. I couldn't do this without you.

Thank you to the Brat Pack, and to our fearless leader Katie. Writing isn't solitary when I know you all are one click away.

Thank you, readers! You're the reason I keep doing this. Thank you for all the messages and emails and hugs when we meet IRL.

xoxo,

About the Author

Valerie Pepper is an incurable optimist and a firm believer in the girl getting the guy, or the guy getting the girl, or the girl getting the girl, or the guy getting the guy, or basically any way it needs to happen to make a real-life happily ever after, even if it takes more than one try.

When she's not writing, you can find her reading, walking, listening to whatever music suits her mood, and hanging out with her family. She's fascinated with the idea of a capsule wardrobe, but loves clothes and shoes and boots far too much to make a real go of it.

She's currently living out her own happily ever after in Birmingham, Alabama, with her family and maaaaaybe too many shoes. Learn more at www.authorvaleriepepper.com.